Down and *Dirty*

a Dare Me novel

Down and *Dirty*

a Dare Me novel

Christine Bell

This book is a work of fiction. Names, characters, places, and incidents are the product of the author's imagination or are used fictitiously. Any resemblance to actual events, locales, or persons, living or dead, is coincidental.

Copyright © 2013 by Christine Bell. All rights reserved, including the right to reproduce, distribute, or transmit in any form or by any means. For information regarding subsidiary rights, please contact the Publisher.

Entangled Publishing, LLC
2614 South Timberline Road
Suite 109
Fort Collins, CO 80525
Visit our website at www.entangledpublishing.com.

Brazen is an imprint of Entangled Publishing, LLC. For more information on our titles, visit www.brazenbooks.com.

Edited by Kerri-Leigh Grady and Heather Howland
Cover design by Heather Howland
Cover art from Shutterstock

Manufactured in the United States of America

First Edition February 2013

*This one is for Heather Howland and Tahra Seplowin for coming up with the "Dare Me" concept, and trusting me to do it justice. *Mwah!* You guys rock!*

Chapter One

Cat Thomas eyed the couple playing tonsil hockey across the black lacquer table and snorted with mock disgust. "Gross. Get a room, would you?"

They broke apart, cheeks flushed, and Cat swallowed a grin. She still wasn't totally used to her best friend and her brother pawing each other, but for all her bitching, she was frigging stoked. They were a great couple—which, to Cat's mind, was as about as common as a two-headed snake—and later this year, she'd be walking down the aisle as Lacey's maid of honor. Again.

"Sorry. Your brother is a perv," Lacey confided with a smile. She slipped off Galen's lap and back onto her own barstool, which was emblazoned with the face of quarterback Peyton Manning. If her friend had to sit on a Manning's face, Peyton was obviously the better option, but the decor of this particular sports bar seemed poorly thought out. Not that it had stopped Cat from spending ten minutes searching for a Tom Brady seat before finally agreeing to sit on Mark Sanchez. He couldn't throw for shit, but he sure was pretty.

"Yeah, I'm the perv," Galen said to his fiancée with a satisfied smirk. "You're the one who had me tie you to th—"

Lacey slapped a hand over his mouth and squealed. "Oh my God, shut up! You're totally going to embarrass your sister."

"Not likely," Cat said. "I won't be thinking too hard about it or anything, because *ew*. But I'm really glad to see he's loosened you up a little." She eyed her laughing friend and shook her head in amazement. Less than a year before, Lacey had found her groom, Marty, in the linen closet of their reception hall, balls-deep in one of her bridesmaids, a lifelong friend of both Cat's and Lacey's. That still made Cat stabby when she thought about it, but she managed to keep her wrath under wraps. Not because of her forgiving nature, but mainly because Lacey was blissfully happy now and settled with her childhood crush, who also happened to be Cat's brother, Galen.

Who woulda thunk it? Not Cat. In fact, the incident between Marty and Lacey had only confirmed what she'd always known: most relationships were far more trouble than they were worth. If Lacey hadn't caught Marty in the act, she'd probably still be with the loser, having the life sucked out of her.

That would never be Cat.

She took a long pull from the lukewarm beer she'd been nursing and glanced around the semi-crowded bar.

Holy hotness.

A man…no, a giant had just stepped into her peripheral vision and derailed all coherent thought. She twisted in her Mark Sanchez chair to get a better look. The guy's head was turned, so she could only see his face in profile, but damn, that and the full-frontal body shot were more than enough. She sized him up with a practiced eye, calling him an easy six-three, two-twenty. He wore a threadbare white T-shirt that should've been as noteworthy as a bowl of oatmeal. Instead, it clung to his chest like it had aspirations of taking over for his skin. Hell, she'd have the same life goal. His chest was a dream, the contours clearly defined by the soft cotton. She could totes cling to him for a night.

In spite of her flight-prone ways, she'd never had a true one-night stand, and it *was* top ten on her bucket list. Maybe...

She took a quick glance at the guy's face to make sure he hadn't caught her staring, then sent her gaze downward to size up the rest of the package.

And speaking of package, *oooh mama*. His jeans were as old as the shirt and had worn down in all the right places, clinging to his thick thighs and what appeared to be a sock... no, a bunch of socks stuffed—

"Shane!" Lacey yelped, launching herself off her stool and scurrying toward him.

No way. There was just no. Frigging. Way.

But apparently there was a way because the sexy behemoth turned to face them full-on, and there he was.

Shane Decker.

He and Galen had met in high school when Galen was a sophomore and Shane was a freshman. They'd bonded over football and had quickly become the best of friends. The four of them had spent a lot of time together the summer before Galen went off to college, so Lacey had stayed in touch with him.

Cat had *not*.

Or at least, not intentionally. Once Galen had gone away, Shane had appointed himself as her official guardian and unofficial conscience. For the majority of her junior year, every time she'd tried to have a little fun, he'd shown up with a disapproving frown and an offer of a ride home.

Except that one night.

The memory—with edges far crisper than they should

have been after all these years—rushed forward, and her face went hot. When Shane met her gaze over Lacey's shoulder, the half-smile stretching his firm lips had her itching to look away, which was silly. She was a grown-ass woman now. She could handle him.

She met his gaze head-on and willed the blood in her cheeks to chillax. It had been a while since she'd seen him, and the years had been kind to the lucky SOB. Generous, even. He looked fantastic, aside from those stormy blue eyes. Like him, they'd always been a little too intense, like he could see inside people's heads and read the thoughts they tried to hide.

"Hey munchkin, how's it going?" He gave Lacey a bear hug, and Cat tried not to stare at his biceps as they flexed.

Galen stood and grinned. "I thought you weren't coming." He yanked his longtime friend into a one-armed man hug. "Did you make it in time to catch any of the fight?"

"Come on. You send me a ticket to your last bout before you retire, and you think I'm not going to show? Not unless there was a monsoon somewhere."

A couple hours before, Galen had defeated Manny Hermosa for the heavyweight belt in a third-round knockout. Even though Shane's job as a search-and-rescue specialist took him all over the world, Cat should've known he would make every effort to get here. He and Galen were like brothers, and that bond had held strong through the years in spite of them living on opposite coasts. Clearly his arrival was a surprise, though. No way would Lacey have left her in the dark on this.

"You were on fire out there. You sure you're ready to hang it up?" Shane asked, giving Galen that searching look that used to make Cat squirm when it was aimed at her.

Galen nodded and slid an arm around Lacey. "I'm old enough to have had a good, long career, and young enough that I'm going to walk away one hundred percent healthy with my melon fully intact. Not something a lot of fighters can say."

Cat doubted that was all there was to Galen's decision, but Shane seemed satisfied with that answer and turned his attention to her. "Mary Catherine."

He tipped his head but didn't move in for an embrace. That didn't surprise her. The handful of times they'd seen each other since he'd left town after high school, they'd circled each other like boxers in the first round of a fight, giving wide berth, sizing up their opponent's strategy. Sure, she covered her anxiety with bravado because...well, because that was how she rolled, but being near him was unnerving at best. He threw her off her game, and she didn't like it one bit.

She took a sip from her glass to whet her suddenly dry whistle. "Hey, Shane."

"Still sewing clothes and breaking hearts?" he asked.

She clenched her hand tighter around her beer, quashing the urge to toss it at him. "Still playing superhero and boring the ladies?" she shot back. Why was it that whenever she was around him, she regressed ten years?

His response came slow, after a long look that made her wish she'd just kept her trap shut for once. "Well, definitely the latter. As for the former, I do what I can."

His self-deprecating response made her feel like a shrew for slapping back at him, but impulse control had never been her strong suit. Especially when it came to Shane Decker. That annoyed her even more, but her brother was eyeballing her hard now. The last thing she needed was another inquisition about why things were always so tense between the two of them. She blew out a sigh and vowed to keep things light and friendly. "Actually, not doing a whole lot of sewing anymore. I have my own line with Nash and Company now. Daytime separates and casual evening wear."

He waited, brows raised, for her to continue, but she

pursed her lips, silently daring him to ask about her breaking hearts again. She'd been getting a lot of flak for her inability to commit lately, so him putting her on blast in front of the two people leading the charge? Made her want to stomp on his foot. She refrained, but it was a close thing.

Light and friendly.

"You planning to stay for the whole weekend?" she asked, trying not to look too interested in his answer. Due to his job, Shane rarely stayed in one place for long. Maybe this was just a quick drive-by show of support for Galen and tomorrow, he'd be on his way again. *Please, God, and thank you.*

"I wasn't sure I was going to be able to get away today until the last minute, so I don't even have a room yet. But no, I'm going to leave tomorrow afternoon." Relief rushed through her, but he continued, "Then I'm actually going to be staying in Rhode Island for a while."

Fuck.

Cat's heart thudded and she could feel Lacey—the only other person who knew about her and Shane's little hookup—staring at her, searching for a reaction. Determined not to give her one, she took a slow, measured sip of her beer.

"You're coming home?" Galen crowed, the delight plain on his face.

Shane nodded, casually snagging one of the stools from the next table and folding his big body onto it. "For a month. It's been a while, and the last couple times I've only managed long weekends, so I took a leave. My parents' thirtieth anniversary is coming up, and Mom's been hounding me about spending more time with the Reign of Terror. I had a ton of unused vacation days, so it seemed like a good time to do it."

The nickname Shane had given his twin five-year-old nieces was a perfect fit. Despite their plump cheeks and wide blue eyes that perpetually avowed innocence, they were a handful. Shane's sister and brother-in-law were awesome parents to the precocious pair, but most days, it was no easy task.

She conjured up her brightest smile and leveled it at Shane. "Yeah, I agree with your mom. More time with the twins is exactly what you need."

Lacey shook her head at Cat and muttered, "You're so bad." She reclaimed her seat across from Cat and turned her attention back to Shane. "So we get to keep you for a while! It's going to be wonderful having you back."

"I'm looking forward to it."

A flicker of something on Shane's face caught Cat's attention. Was there something more to this leave of absence than he was letting on? Maybe there was, but it was none of her business. She needed to focus on staying out of his way for the next month. It wouldn't be so bad. She'd run into him around town and probably a couple times at Galen and Lacey's, but she could use work as an excuse to stay scarce until he was safely back in California.

"And we're really glad you were able to make it for the fight. I know it goes without saying, but if they don't have any rooms left tonight, you can bunk with us," Lacey offered with a smile.

"That's okay," Shane said. "If not here, they'll have one at Caesar's or something. No worries."

Galen gave him two thumbs up paired with a grin that was all male. "Thanks, buddy."

Lacey smacked his arm and blushed. "You're going to make him feel unwelcome."

"Babe, I've followed the prefight no-sex regimen for ten days now. I'm pretty sure something's going to pop if I have to go another night. We can make him feel welcome tomorrow. Or," he glanced at his watch-free wrist, "in like fourteen minutes if we go up and start now."

"Be still my heart," Lacey said, face still flaming.

Cat rolled her eyes and Shane barked out a laugh.

"Seriously, though, if you can't find a place..." Galen's expression was sincere. In spite of his razzing, Cat knew—hell, they all knew—he would give his friend the shirt off his back if Shane needed it. They were like family, and family took care of one another.

Guilt pricked at her. Her brother had just won the last fight of his career. A career that Cat wasn't certain he was truly ready to give up. Surely he deserved to spend a little quality time alone with his fiancée to celebrate?

Lacey cleared her throat, eying her pointedly, and Cat glared back.

All right, all right. "Let's not get all in a tizz," Cat said, the world's fakest smile stretching her lips. "First, let's see if we can get him a room." She shot off another unspoken prayer, this one complete with mental gesticulation for good measure, and continued. "If not, I have two queen beds in mine. He can stay with me. No big deal."

No. Big. Deal.

Except when Shane looked at her, it felt like a big deal. The sound of the jukebox faded away, muffled by the beat of her heart in her ears, and the memory came again, unbidden. The drag of that mouth along her neck. The warm water lapping against her breasts. A full moon, fat in the sky, lighting his face. Clenched jaw, bodies rocking, Shane pulling away, with a whispered *no*.

"Yes!" Lacey smacked her hand on the table.

Cat jerked back, tearing her gaze from Shane's to face her friend.

Lacey's eyes were bright with excitement. "Awesome idea. Now that's settled, let's get another drink." She leaned back with a satisfied smile and raised her hand to flag down the blonde cocktail waitress in a purple bustier. "Shane, beer for you?"

"Sure." His voice was suspiciously husky and Cat wondered for a crazy instant if the whole mind-reading thing wasn't so far-fetched, but he seemed to recover quickly, turning his attention to Lacey. "Whatever's seasonal on tap is good."

The waitress took the rest of their orders and then made her way to the bar. The others chatted amiably about Shane's job and updated him on the latest family news and town gossip. Cat took the time to regroup, and when the waitress returned with the drinks, she was back on track. Shane was there. Big frigging deal. Whatever had transpired between them was old news. So why, all these years later, was she still acting like a teenager after a Bieber sighting? It was going to stop, here and now.

She threw back her shoulders, ready to dive into the discussion and behave like her witty, charming self, but she was saved the effort when some fans approached their table asking Galen for an autograph. Once the floodgate was opened, there was no closing it, and over the next hour, dozens of people stopped by for a picture or a high five. Her brother handled it so well and seemed genuinely honored each and every time, which made them love him even more. Invariably, once the female sect realized that Galen was very taken, they turned hot eyes on Shane and asked if he was a fighter, too.

"Nope. Just a regular Joe," he'd drawl.

The most recent group—this one, all ladies—was clearly out for a good time and didn't mind Shane's lack of pro-athlete status. One dark-haired chick separated herself from the pack and boldly dragged a stool up to sit beside him. "More like a G.I. Joe. Where'd you get all those muscles?"

Her skirt was so short that Cat caught a flash of rhinestones that were either appliquéd onto the front of a flesh-colored thong or part of the girl's attempt at vajazzling. Cat's professional curiosity required her to investigate further—even if she didn't design underwear—so she squinted hard, half-tempted to squat down for a proper look. If she eyeballed the girl's lady parts any harder, she was going to feel obligated to buy her dinner or something.

When she finally looked up, she found Shane staring at her with a bemused smile. She turned away, cheeks hot. So much for playing it cool.

"Well, Joe? You gonna tell me where you got all these fine muscles?" the vajazzler pressed, pouting as she leaned into him.

"Just like to stay fit, is all."

Cat looked at him hard. Was it her imagination or was he leaning away from those gargantuan breasts? Interesting.

The woman seemed to note that, too, and after a few more halfhearted attempts at flirtation, stood with a defeated sigh. "Well, this bar's pretty dead. We're going to find some action. Nice meeting y'all."

She tottered away on her knockoff Pradas and Cat turned to face Shane. "What's up with that?"

"What's up with what?"

"Most guys would have jumped at the opportunity to make some time with her. You have a girlfriend back in Cali or something?"

"Nope. I'm just…selective." His gaze drifted from her face downward, and Cat's breath hitched. How could such an innocuous word seem so suggestive coming from those lips? Lips that she would love to—

She froze, slamming the door on that thought, quick. Even if she did think he was sexy in an overly intense and annoying way, and even if he did want to pick up where they'd left off all those years ago—which he surely didn't—a fling between them would cause nothing but problems in the long run. She didn't need a protector all up in her business and he didn't need a…what was it he'd called her that night at the lake? Right. A "spoiled pain in the ass with a death wish" messing up his neat little life, even for a little while.

She'd broken eye contact with him and was about to excuse herself to run her heated mug under the ladies' room faucet when Galen let out a groan.

"Anybody hungry?" He rubbed his stomach and frowned. "I feel like I haven't eaten in a week."

"Lacey and I ordered a couple appetizers while we were waiting for you to shower and ice down," Cat said.

"Yeah, we're all set," Lacey agreed. "I ate my weight in tapas. Want to order something? Kitchen is still open, I think. Want me to get a menu?"

Shane nodded. "I had peanuts on the flight and that's about it, so I'm starved."

"I'm hungry for man-food, babe," Galen said. "I'm not interested in salmon mousse with a bunch of field greens, or tapas. I want to go to Johnny Rockets and get a big, fat burger and some fries." He rubbed his stomach again, this time with a longing expression.

"It's the middle of the night," Lacey said, nose wrinkling. "If I eat that it'll sit in my stomach like a rock and I won't be able to sleep. You guys go. Me and Cat will hang here and have another drink before bed." She looked to Cat for approval.

"Sounds good to me. I don't want to go traipsing all over town in these heels anyway." She poked a finger at her kickin' crimson stilettos and wagged her foot.

Shane slid a glance downward and then met her gaze. "I could give you a piggyback if you want." His voice was low enough that she had to strain to hear him over the music, and his words sent a pulse of heat through her.

"I'm okay, thanks," she said, too quickly, before reclaiming her cool. "Me and Lacey will stick here for a bit."

"Won't you be lonely without me?" Galen leaned forward and tucked a strand of hair behind Lacey's ear.

She playfully swatted his hand away. "Nope. Your sister is good company. Besides, I'll see you in the room a little later."

"You going to wait up for me?"

The sizzling look between her brother and her best friend made Cat turn away, but not before she saw Lacey's cheeks flush and her eyes sparkle.

"You guys are so gross, even if I was hungry before, I'm not anymore," she announced and stood. "Come on, let's grab the waitress and order another while these boys stuff their faces."

While Lacey kissed Galen like he was going off to war, Cat made a show of picking some lint off her black pencil skirt, giving it the stank eye. It was a prototype, and after only two wears it was already pilling. She made a mental note to talk to manufacturing about other fabric options before it went to production.

"How about you?" Shane asked softly, derailing her thoughts. He stepped in closer until she had to crane her neck to see his face. "You going to wait up for me?"

Jesus, he was handsome. "Wh-what?" Blerg. Had she really just stammered like that? She was Cat fucking Thomas. Successful designer. Daredevil extraordinaire. A goddamn force to be reckoned with. She was *so* not going to allow some stick-in-the-mud to get a rise out of her just because he touched her boobies one time almost a decade ago. She cleared her throat and raised a brow at him. "And why, pray tell, would I wait up for you, Decker?"

"Well, Mary Catherine," he said, the smile in his voice belying his earnest expression, "if I can't get a room, and you haven't offered me a key, how else am I supposed to get in?"

Damn. "Right. Of course." She took an instinctive step back, desperate for some space, and reached for her purse. "You take my key and I'll get another one at the front desk," she said. She plucked the card from her bag and held it out to him. "Number 1248, Garden Tower. Make sure you go by the front desk before you eat to see if they have an open room first. And stop calling me Mary Catherine," she added, not caring that she sounded like a petulant child.

He popped off a salute and gave her a mocking smile. "Will do." His fingers brushed hers as he reached for the keycard, and she steeled herself. She'd always loved his hands, even in high school, even before he'd ever laid them on her. The hands of a man. Strong and hard, ready to throw a football or pull in an anchor, but equally capable of sliding ever so gently over a hip…

"Thanks," he said, tugging the key from her death grip before stepping back. "I'll have Galen text you one way or the other so I don't startle you." He turned to follow her brother, who had already started for the door.

Cat watched them walk away, heart pounding, eyes glued to Shane's ass. The mental strip-down she was giving him wasn't exclusive to that region, though. Where had those shoulders come from? He'd been in shape when they were young, but this? This was out of control. She blinked and sucked in a deep breath. "I don't know what the hell is wrong with me," she muttered, more to herself than anything.

Lacey followed her gaze. "I can help you there. You're impulsive, *realllly* short, like almost stumpy, and you've got a potty mouth."

"Thanks. I feel much better now."

Lacey slid back onto her stool and patted the one next to her that Galen had vacated. "Seriously, though, there's nothing wrong with you. You're perfect. But I'm guessing the Shane thing got you freaked?"

Cat hopped onto the seat and shook her head. "No. Yes." She scrubbed a hand over her face and groaned. "Shit, hell if I know anymore. It's just so…awkward whenever he's around."

"Doesn't that tell you something?"

"Yeah. It tells me that I should try harder to not be around him. Which I've done a really great job of until tonight."

Lacey just shrugged. "Don't look at me. I knew your

brother invited him, but Shane told us he couldn't make it. How was I supposed to know he was going to surprise us?"

"You weren't. It's not your fault. I'm just not looking forward to playing 'Dodge Shane' for a month when we get back home. Not to mention the fifty-fifty shot of having to shack up with him tonight." She absently traced a circle of condensation on the table with her pinky, willing herself not to think about having to sleep with Shane in the next bed.

"Well, I think it's great." Lacey said, and crossed her arms over her chest. "It's high time you dealt with this. I want us all to be able to hang out while Shane is home, like we used to, and tonight is the perfect time to clear the air with him."

"And how am I supposed to do that? I'm pretty sure most of it's one-sided, and the parts that aren't are probably in my head. So what do I say? 'Hey Shane, let's talk about that time we almost banged a billion years ago, and why I remember it like it was yesterday in spite of the fact that I can barely stand you.'"

Lacey drew back and gasped. "I knew that was it! That's what makes you so uncomfortable around him. Not that it happened, but that you want a repeat performance."

"First of all, it was certainly not a 'performance.' It was a prelude at best. And second, no I don't." At Lacey's dubious stare, she amended, "Or if I do, it's only because of the curiosity. You know how when someone takes a bite of something and says 'Ew, this is gross! Take a bite,' and you know it's going to be bad, but you have to try it anyway? Like that."

"You didn't seem to think it was gross that night. In fact, I recall you saying that his hands were like magic and—"

Cat cupped her palms over her ears and groaned. "Ugh, I know what I said. I was a melodramatic teenage girl. I also thought *From Justin to Kelly* should have won an Oscar. What did I know? Anyways, you're missing the point of my analogy."

"That's because it was a stupid analogy. I think you owe it to yourself to figure out what all the fuss in your head has been about."

She pulled her hands away and laid them on the table faceup. "Look, I know it's your fondest wish that Shane and I get married and have a pile of kids and get a minivan so we can be besties married to besties, but that's not going to happen. You know that, right, Lace?"

Her friend nodded, but not convincingly. "Yeah. I'm just wondering if maybe this has been the holdup with you and other guys. You had this amazing night with Shane that never resolved itself and since then, no one has measured up. Every guy you date, you dump after discovering some silly, made-up flaws."

"They're not made up," Cat protested. "Some of them are—"

Lacey shut her down with a talk-to-the-hand. "What about Steve? Pushing someone away because they don't get your Monty Python references isn't normal."

"Bring out yer dead!" Cat quipped with a weak smile, and slumped in her seat, trying not to get too defensive.

Lacey shook her head, exasperation plain on her face. "What about Ty? Or Griff? He was so nice."

She bolted upright, nearly knocking over her beer. "Whoa, wait a second. Who could date Griff long-term? He used the phrase 'That's my motto' like five times a day. 'Go hard or go home, that's my motto.' 'You only live once, that's my motto.' 'Shoot for the stars and you're bound to hit one, that's my motto.' Jesus, Griff, pick a fucking motto, am I right? It was ridiculous." Even as she said it, she could feel her cheeks getting warm. Maybe Griff wasn't the only one who was ridiculous.

Lacey's lips twitched, but she held strong. "I'm serious here. I'm not saying any of these guys have been your soul mate, but I *am* saying that you'll never know if you don't let them in a little."

"If they had their way, I'd be letting him in a lot, if you

catch my drift." Her friend's cheeks went pink and Cat chuckled. "For all the changes in you, it makes me proud that I can still get you to blush."

Lacey sniffed and folded the bar napkin into a neat rectangle and set it next to her beer glass. "Stop trying to derail the conversation." The waitress passed by and Lacey held up two fingers, gesturing at their empty glasses before turning her focus back on Cat.

"So what do you suggest, Lace? I should just ignore my instincts and stick around when someone is rubbing me the wrong way? Because that's what it sounds like." She tried to keep the edge out of her tone, but judging by her friend's wounded expression, she'd missed the mark a little.

Lacey lifted her chin. "Nope. What you should do is make sure you're not throwing the baby out with the bathwater."

"That's the stupidest expression ever. Who throws out a baby? Like, 'Oh, oops. Didn't see you there, li'l fella.' Not to mention, you'd think they'd cry when they landed and you'd catch your mistake in time to scoop it back into the bath."

Lacey's eyes went kind of evil and she poked Cat's arm, hard.

Damn, Galen really had toughened her up.

"Stop. Deflecting. It's fine to be like Shane said. Selective. It's not fine for you to run every guy off within two months over some perceived flaw."

"I'm not taking dating advice from Old Killjoy Decker. Even in high school, when *everyone* was being irresponsible and having fun, he was busy looking for parades to crap on. I'm sure that hasn't changed and he's still about as exciting as a kiddie roller coaster." And seeing as how Cat typically selected vacation destinations based on the proximity of the best amusement park, this was the highest of insults.

A crease marred Lacey's brow and she gave her golden head a shake. "I never understood that. He's the most fun, interesting guy I know—besides your brother, of course. And gorgeous to boot. How could you possibly think he's boring?"

"Maybe the way he tried to corral me my entire junior year of high school like I was some wayward cow and he was the ranch's most enthusiastic farmhand?"

The waitress came by with their beers, and Cat leaned aside to make room. It gave her a moment to think, and she decided grudgingly that maybe boring wasn't the right word for Shane. An image of that sexy, soul-searching stare sent a bolt of heat through her. Sexy? It wasn't sexy. It was…invasive. And annoying.

And sexy.

When the waitress strolled away, Lacey held up a hand. "The super-hot professional hero with an amazing work ethic and one of the best men I've ever known is boring. Fine. You are officially hopeless. Nobody is good enough for you. So, great, you'll get exactly what you've been working toward your whole life."

Cat knew for sure she didn't want to hear the rest of this. In fact, maybe it was time to hit the slots—

"A life alone."

Cat winced.

"Hah! You flinched!" Lacey shouted, stabbing a triumphant finger in Cat's direction. "You try to act so tough, but you don't want to be alone forever, do you?"

"You didn't just discover plutonium, genius, so calm down. It's not that shocking. Who wants to be alone forever? I just haven't found the ri—"

"You haven't even tried. Twenty-five's in the rearview mirror, and you've never had a relationship last longer than ninety days. That's sad."

Maybe it was. But it seemed to her that relationships were a constant drain. Even when the getting was good, one person always ended up compromising. Most of the time, they gave up so much of themselves they became someone else entirely. That's why she mainly hung out with guys who were willing to give a little, get a little, and let her live the rest of her life on her terms. When things got too serious, she walked away. Maybe it was time to take a harder look at the cycle. Not to give herself over completely, but to find a guy who wanted the same things she did.

Cat plucked a bar napkin off the table and began absently rolling the edges. "Okay, so what then? I should propose to Shane so I don't die alone?"

Lacey's soft features went tight. "Don't be a smart-ass. Of course not, I'm just saying that you shouldn't be so damned hasty."

Cat took a sip of her beer and mulled it over.

"In fact," Lacey said, her tone eulogy-serious, "I dare you."

Cat gaped at her friend, noting the challenge in her eyes that looked so out of place. "Dare me to what?"

"I triple-dog dare you to explore this Shane thing and see if it's just a case of nostalgia. If it is, no harm, no foul. You can get some closure and move on. And if it's not? Maybe you can actually admit to yourself that you have some feelings for him that need to be dealt with."

Lacey looked pleased as punch, so sure that Cat would take the bait. What did she think, Cat was an idiot? So easily led that she would just cave and—

Shane's mocking half-grin flashed in front of her eyes. *Still sewing clothes and breaking hearts?*

Maybe she was, but who was he to judge? Lacey was right. The deed couldn't possibly live up to the hype she'd built up in her head. Maybe if she got him out of her system, she could focus on finding a guy more suited to her lifestyle long-term. Someone fun and easy.

Someone exactly not like Shane.

A vision of his face, those cutting blue eyes drilling into

her, ran through her mind, and common sense flooded back in. "Nope. This is one dare I'm going to have to pass on."

Lacey's face fell a little, but she nodded. "Okay, well, you have the month to think about it. And if not Shane, at least consider opening up to someone and allowing yourself to connect before you dump the guy. I only want you to be happy, Cat."

Despite the seriousness in Lacey's big brown eyes, Cat couldn't contain the laughter bubbling up. "We must be in Crazy Town right now. What are the odds that you would end up being the one to dare me to do something this trip?"

Since grade school, she'd coerced Lacey to go along with her, daring her to do all sorts of nutty stuff, from dyeing her hair green to jumping out of a plane, but this was the first time the shoe had been on the other foot.

Lacey's lips twitched into a grudging smile. "Pretty low, I guess. In fact, we probably have a better chance of winning at the slots."

"Amen to that." She clinked her glass to Lacey's and took a swig of beer. As the icy liquid poured down her throat, Lacey tugged her cell phone from her pants pocket and peered down at the screen.

"A text from Galen. No rooms, so Shane will be staying with you."

As Cat digested that news, she half-expected a bell to toll. Was that a sign of some sort? Of course not. It stood to reason that the hotel was booked to capacity due to the big fight. It had no bearing on her and Shane at all, except that they'd be in the same room. She'd stayed in the same room with him dozens of times on trips to the Thomas family cottage, so this was no biggie.

So why couldn't she shake the sense of foreboding pressing on her like an anvil?

Chapter Two

Cat Thomas.

Shane waited for Galen to finish signing an autograph and tossed some bills onto the Formica table, wondering once again if he'd made a mistake by coming back east. When Galen had invited him, it had been a no-brainer. He'd intended for it to be a short trip, a day or two in Atlantic City, a day or two to visit the family up north, and then back to California. But the past few months had been a wake-up call for him, and he was starting to think that maybe life was too short and fragile to be this far from the people he loved. It was time to go home for a good long while. Maybe even for good, if his transfer went through.

"Ready to rock-and-roll?" Galen asked, elbowing him in the ribs as he passed.

"Yeah, man, I'm shot from that red-eye flight."

"You?" Galen asked, his eyes popping comically wide. "I spent half my night getting punched in the face."

"Don't bullshit me. I was there, and if you got hit more than ten times, you can punch *me* in the face."

Galen shrugged, waving to their waitress as they exited the little fifties-style diner. "Maybe so, but that guy's fists are like two Buicks wrapped in bacon. That shit hurts."

"Remind me to feel sorry for you later when you're lying on your piles of money and your gorgeous fiancée is rubbing all your aches away."

His friend laughed at that, the kind of laugh that told Shane the bastard knew exactly how lucky he was. Good thing, too. If not, Shane would have made it his personal mission to remind him.

They made their way to the elevators, and his thoughts drifted back to Cat. It had been almost three years since he'd seen her last. He'd hoped by now she'd have grown up enough to want a real man, someone strong enough to go toe-to-toe with her. Or if not, then at least he'd have grown out of wanting to be that man. That maybe this time, when he saw her, he wouldn't have the inane urge to throw her over his shoulder and carry her to his cave.

He couldn't have been more wrong on the last count. If anything, he wanted her even more. She'd always been hot and confident, even at sixteen, but as she got older, she got better and better. He'd never seen someone five-foot-nothing take up so much space. Her energy and charisma made her the biggest person in the room, and it was an effort not to watch her every animated move. Too bad she was such a chickenshit.

Shane shook his head. "So have you guys picked a date for the wedding yet?"

"Nope, but we're thinking summertime."

"Best time to have it in Rhode Island. That's one thing I'm not looking forward to—spending the next month in the nut-shrinking cold." They stepped onto the elevator and Galen punched in their floor number. He cleared his throat, and strived to keep his tone casual. "How's Cat been doing? Got a guy at home or still a lone wolf?"

Galen shook his head. "Not yet. She's a tough nut, that one. But I gotta be honest, there've been a couple real douchebags lately, and I'm glad she's not settling for just anyone. My only concern is that she'll toss the good ones away as quick as the bad. She's got commitment issues."

While the last part wasn't great news for him, the first half of Galen's admission had him breathing a sigh of relief. No guy. At least he had a chance then.

The elevator doors slid open, and he and Galen stepped out. "This way. We're in the same wing."

When they reached Galen's room first, his friend turned to face him. "Breakfast tomorrow?"

"I'm going to try to get a solid seven, but call me when you guys wake up, and if I answer I'll meet you for eggs before I leave."

"Sounds good. You're three doors down." He thrust his chin down the long hallway and slipped his key in the lock. "Just a warning, it's about to get crazy in here. You may want to wear earplugs." A lethal grin lit Galen's face, and Shane rolled his eyes.

"Sure thing, asshole."

Galen's chuckle echoed behind him as Shane made his way to Cat's room. Just as he was opening the door, Lacey's feminine laugh spilled down the hallway to join Galen's. Good for him. His lady did wait up. So did that mean Cat was here? His pulsed kicked up. Lacey's laughter was cut short when Shane closed the door behind him. One light on, no one home. Maybe she'd stopped off to gamble for a while before coming up.

He took in the opulent surroundings, eyeing the two queen beds draped in green and gold. Cat's hair would look like fire against those colors, like New England in the fall. He groaned, tossed the key and his wallet onto the dresser, and headed for the bathroom. A shower first, to clear his head, and then he'd figure out how to deal with this damn woman.

An hour later, he bit back a curse. The very blankets he'd been admiring were now his own personal instruments of torture and still no Cat. He growled, kicking at the sheets strangling his legs like a straitjacket, and rolled off the bed to yank them from beneath the mattress. Who could sleep like that? He shook the bedding out to cover the bed loosely, then climbed beneath the layers, tugging them up over his shoulder as his thoughts drifted back to Cat.

Maybe that's why she couldn't settle down. Maybe that was how relationships made her feel. Hotel-tucked. Trapped. And the tighter the tuck, the more panicked she got. Whatever the case, if her response to his little "heartbreaker" jab was any indication, nothing had changed on her end either. She still wasn't in the market for a serious relationship. And didn't that fucking blow. Although it was better than showing up after all this time and finding her madly in love with someone else.

Just the thought soured the burgers in his stomach. Thank God she wasn't. From what he'd gathered from Galen, she was definitely single.

But where the hell was she?

Shane stared at the whorls in the ceiling and then rolled to his side, shifting a bleary eye to the empty bed next to his again. It had been two hours since they'd left her and Lacey at the bar. Was she going to just stay out all night in an effort to avoid him, or was she going to put on her big-girl pants at some point and come back to the room? Either way was okay with him. He had at least a month and if everything went according to plan, he'd have all the time in the world to get her to see things his way. He briefly considered going down to the poker room rather than stewing, but twenty-four hours with only the fitful nap on the plane in the way of sleep hit him all at once and his lids finally drifted closed.

His last waking thought was of Cat in the lake, a damp, red curl obscuring one green eye, her siren's smile mocking him.

...

Cat smothered another semi-hysterical laugh and stepped into the elevator. She pressed the number twelve, then, on whim, frantically batted all the other numbers in between like she was playing Whac-A-Mole.

Now you're just stalling.

She couldn't argue with herself there. She'd definitely been stalling. After walking Lacey back to her room, she'd felt a sudden burning desire to play the slots. Two hours, four drinks and three hundred dollars later, she was tired enough that her eyes were stinging, but it took all her courage to leave the casino. Scared to be in the same room alone with Shane Decker. Because, after six months of self-imposed celibacy and almost a decade of wondering, she didn't know if she'd be able to keep her hands to herself. And after the second drink—or was it the third?—she'd started thinking that maybe Lacey was right. Not about the "opening up and giving a guy a real chance" thing. Not happening. But the whole "getting Shane out of her system" thing had seemed like a better idea with every sip.

The desire had been too deeply buried to make the official print version, but if she was being totally honest with herself, finishing what she'd started with Shane was hella-high on her mental bucket list. Now, though, with nothing but an elevator ride and a short hallway between them, she was seriously considering knocking on Lacey and Galen's door and asking if she could crash on their couch.

Because what if he turned her away? Again.

"Stop it, you chicken."

She was overthinking. And overthinking was Lacey's bag, not hers. Cat Thomas was a doer, and she was so doing this. Her brain reeled back to the thought of Shane in his snug T-shirt, and she allowed herself to embrace it. It was time to put this thing with him to bed. And after that? He'd go back to California at the end of the month and everything would be fine.

After stopping at every floor, the elevator finally reached twelve, and she stepped out. She made her way down the hall on trembling legs, arriving at her door too soon. Another chuckle threatened and she bit her lip. The pleasant buzz she'd been working on was disappearing fast in the wake of her nerves, and she briefly considered heading back down for one more nip of liquid courage.

"Wuss," she muttered under her breath. She was done acting like a virgin on her wedding night. She was a grown, powerful woman asserting her sexuality. And while Shane may not want to want her, there was no hiding the masculine appreciation in his eyes earlier.

With a toss of her head, she reached in her bag, bypassing the four-pack of condoms she'd picked up at the hotel drugstore earlier, and palmed her keycard. She slid it slowly into the slot then pulled it out. The resulting *snick* reverberated in her head like a shot. Surely it hadn't been loud enough to wake him, had it? If she had to face him first she'd never be able to go through with this.

Before her courage could flag any further, she opened the door and stepped into the room, then closed it softly behind her. It was pitch black and silent, except for the sound of Shane's low, even breathing. Thank God.

She paused, briefly considering whether to change into her nightclothes before getting in or just stripping down. The image of climbing into Shane's bed in her Star Trek T-shirt and ratty boxer shorts had her choking back more laughter.

She'd have to go with option B.

She felt around for the dresser, then laid the keycard on top. She toed off the stilettos she'd had on all night and made quick work of her blouse and skirt. When she was down to bra and panties, another wave of nerves hit, and she stopped. They could deal with those once she was in the bed with him. She reached into her purse and pulled out the box of condoms. Then, on tiptoe, she padded across the carpet, moving at a snail's pace in an effort to get across the room, toes unstubbed. When she reached the bed closest to the door, she laid a gentle hand on the covers. Cold and still neatly tucked in. Her heart thumped faster as she faced the second bed, hand outstretched.

He was there. She could feel the heat pouring off him. An earthy, male scent permeated the air, and she moved closer, letting her hand drift down. For the first time since she'd decided to do this, a bolt of pure desire sliced through her, leaving her doubts in tatters. Her fingertips came into contact with warm skin, and she drew back with a gasp. Wrong side of the bed, but luckily, his breathing stayed steady as she hurried around to the other side. She laid the condoms on the bedside table, then pulled back the covers, breath suspended, and climbed in. The sheets on her side were chilled, but she suppressed a shiver as she waited to see if she'd disturbed him.

Still nothing. *Sweet.*

The rush of victory and adrenaline coursed through her, and she rolled closer, absorbing his heat, until she was pressed flush against his broad back. Her nipples peaked instantly, and she plastered herself closer, relishing the sensation. Damn, he was big. Bigger than she'd remembered. Shane shifted restlessly, slinging his muscular arm back to cup her ass and tug her more firmly against him. A low, male groan of approval followed, and he gave her bottom a squeeze.

A quiver of awareness snaked through her at his confident

touch. Such a small thing, but for some reason it terrified her. What if they really were *that* good together?

She drew away, the sense of foreboding from earlier returning with a vengeance, but that hard, male hand slid down the back of her thigh and up again to cup her ass, derailing her thoughts. She wrapped her arm around his waist and traced her fingers over his six-pack abs, half-wishing she'd had the balls to turn on the lights so she could get a look at them. His stomach tensed beneath her questing hand, and she let her fingers trail lower, over the narrow strip of hair leading downward. When she hit his underwear and found the broad head of his cock distended past the waistband, her heart hammered double-time. She ran her thumb over the silken skin and swallowed a moan. He felt so good. It was almost enough to make her rush things and jump right on him.

Almost.

She slipped her hand beneath the cotton and closed it over his long, thick shaft, not bothering to hide her murmur of approval. Big and hard all over. This decision was looking better by the minute. Shane shifted his hips, arching more fully into her grasp.

His muttered "Fuck, yeah," made her want to collapse with relief, so different from the *"No, Cat. We have to stop"* from last time. The hand on her ass massaged her, urging her to grind against his back. Tingles radiated from between her thighs, and she couldn't help but pulse her hips in response, suddenly aching for more pressure. She stroked him once from base to tip, light and teasing, and he groaned, his voice gravelly with sleep and need.

Then, a second later, she found herself flat on her back and he was going down, down...

• • •

Cat.

Shane's whole body cranked to eleven, and hot blood pumped to his cock as her warm scent assailed him. Lush, spicy, and a little wild, like oranges and the Orient. That soft, supple body he'd imagined his hands all over a thousand times pressed against him. With a dream this hot, he would kill any motherfucker who dared wake him. It wouldn't be the first time she'd invaded his sleep. It would, however, be the most vivid. So vivid, almost—

His dream temptress arched against him then, and his brain short-circuited when his lips brushed a lace-covered nipple. He drew the stiff peak into his mouth and she bowed her back, purring low in her throat. He trailed his hand over her rib cage, down the flat expanse of her stomach until he reached the tiny scrap of silk covering her wet heat. Her whispered pleas spurred him on and he yanked, the cloth coming away in his hand. He tossed it aside and released her nipple to press sucking kisses down her side, desperate to taste what he'd uncovered. When he reached her hip, he couldn't resist the full curve and nipped her sharply with his teeth. Her cry was one of pleasure, and he groaned, torn between the need to explore her some more and the need to feel her come against his mouth.

He slipped a hand between her thighs and the decision was made. The skin was like satin, with only a thin strip of down covering her. Her plumped clit pouted against the heel of his palm, and he pressed in, rewarded by a rush of heat and her moan. His cock jerked, and he slid farther down the bed to kiss her there. She was stock-still beneath him except for her thighs trembling. He settled in closer to run his tongue up her slick crease. When he reached her clit, he closed his lips over it and rubbed rhythmically with his tongue.

"Oh my God," she groaned, quivering against him, legs falling open wide. He tested her readiness, then slid two fingers deep, pressing them into her wet warmth. She arched toward him, hips pulsing restlessly.

"Deeper," she begged.

Her request made his cock surge and he complied, sliding deeper, working in and out in a slow, steady rhythm, all the while sucking, licking, reveling in her taste. She thrust her hips up, grinding against his face as he increased the pressure of his mouth. He went at her with a ravenous hunger, driven to consume, until she writhed beneath him frantically. It felt like forever and no time at all when, dimly, he heard her broken cries, and she tensed.

"Please, stay with me," she moaned, holding him tight to her pussy as she pulsed and twitched against his mouth. Her sweet, hot juices bathed his tongue, and he couldn't contain his growl of satisfaction. If he didn't get inside her in the next thirty seconds, he was going to explode. When her thighs relaxed, he didn't waste a second, yanking off his boxers and covering her still trembling body with his own.

She pressed him back with a staying hand and stretched toward the bedside table. "Condom," she murmured breathlessly.

The word hit him like a locomotive.

Condom.

In the dozens—no, hundreds—of sex dreams he'd had in his life starring Cat, not a single one had ever involved a condom. The scrape of lace as she wriggled against his chest penetrated the sensual fog and sent another warning signal blaring. He enjoyed sexy bras as much as the next guy, but his fantasies almost exclusively featured Cat buck naked.

Total exhaustion had left him addled, but it was clear now. This was the real deal. Cat Thomas, wet and wanting, thighs spread wide under him, was waiting for him to slide home and make her scream. He didn't know what had changed her mind about him, but it was about fucking time.

In the utter blackness, on the precipice of fantasy becoming reality, every sound seemed amplified. The tear of foil, his own heaving breaths as her sure fingers worked the condom over his cock, her gasp as he tipped his hips forward, testing her readiness.

"Yess," she hissed, clutching at his hips, dragging him deeper, inch by inch. "I want it all."

The need was so keen it made him dizzy, and he gave up the fight, filling her tight sheath in one sure thrust. Deep, so deep she whimpered against his shoulder, and he started to pull back. Dial down the intensity. She was so small, and he—

Her teeth clamped down hard on his shoulder, and her nails dug into his lower back, urging him on. Begging him wordlessly not to stop.

She dropped her head back to the pillow and pulsed her hips against his, faster and faster. "I'm so close. Just…"

He'd wanted to tease, to play, to cool her back down only to fan those flames even higher, but he was so far gone. She whispered another plea, but it came on a hiccup, and he froze, buried deep in her clutching heat, primed for release. His breath sawed in and out of his lungs with the effort of his restraint. He peered at the clock. Almost 4:00 a.m. Had she been drinking this whole time? "Cat, I—"

"Don't." Her tone was high and reedy, ripe with want. "Don't you dare. Fucking. Stop." She strained against him, wild and desperate for something only he could provide.

He tried to think clearly, to fight off the instinct to propel them both into oblivion. Then her body squeezed over him, sucking at him, luring him toward an orgasm he could no more deny her than he could himself, and all coherent thought ceased. Blood roaring in his ears, he pulled back and plunged forward again, gripping her hips tight, the pressure of his own release clawing at him like a beast demanding satisfaction.

"Yeah, yeah, just like that," she chanted, stretching

beneath him, her whole body tensing.

Just like that. It was all so fucking perfect. But did she even know what she was doing or who she was with?

"Say my name." His voice was raw and low. "Say it, Cat," he demanded, snapping his hips against hers in steady, hard thrusts. "You know it's me, so fucking say it."

Her head tossed on the pillow and she moaned, "Damn, ah, Shane! I—I—oh God." Her body clasped him tight and fluttered, clutching and releasing as she came hard around his cock.

Triumph coursed through him, sending him hurtling over the edge, and his body bucked, hot liquid pooling in his balls before pumping into her. Her body milked him dry, the waves of ecstasy leaving him shuddering. For a long moment, he stayed poised over her, his pulse pounding so loud it was a wonder he could hear anything else. Because he'd just had sex with Cat Thomas. And it had been damned good. Excellent, really. But something told him that things were about to go downhill fast.

He rolled to the side to take care of the condom, and before he could roll back, she'd sat up and swung her legs over the side of the bed. Soldiering through the stab in his gut at her rush to get away from him, he kept his voice low.

"So that's it? You going to run now, Cat?"

Chapter Three

Hells yeah, she was going to run. Shane had just turned her ass upside down, and her head was reeling. The whole have-sex-to-get-him-out-of-her-system plan had failed miserably. She should have known better. She'd read her fair share of romance novels, and none of that shit ever worked out the way it was supposed to. But she'd prided herself on not being one of those women.

Yet here she was.

She stood in the darkness and willed her shaky legs to move. She had to get away from him before she said or did something even stupider than she'd already done. After taking a few slow breaths to steady herself, she spoke. "I'm not running. I'm just going to take a hot shower, change into my pajamas, and get into my own bed. That's hardly running." The iciness she'd injected into her response didn't have quite the bite she'd hoped since her voice was still a bit shaky from the smoking-hot sex they'd just had, but she pressed on. "Is that a problem?"

"Nope. Not once we've finished our little talk." The

mattress squeaked, and a second later the bedside lamp flickered on. She flinched at the sudden brightness.

"Jesus, warn somebody before you do that." She felt blindly around for the sheets and held an armload in front of her, the modesty feeling a little foolish since he'd been inside her less than a minute before. She backed her way toward the corner of the room where her clothes lay on the floor.

Through her squinted eyes she could see him, reclined on the bed, naked and watching her. "Can you close your eyes, please?" she groaned, more annoyed at herself for staring at those glorious shoulders than she was at him.

He did as she asked. She tugged on her blouse and wrapped the sheet around her like a skirt. "Okay, you can open them."

"I'm pretty sure I get it, but you want to tell me what just happened here?" he asked, crossing his thick arms over his chest. The motion drew her gaze to the black Japanese symbol on his shoulder, and she again found herself struggling for words. She wouldn't have figured boring Shane for a tattoo guy. Although, she wouldn't have figured him for the kind of guy who had just done...that with her, either. If she'd known it would be so primal, she never would have done it.

Damn it, Shane, you were supposed to bore me.

"I just figured it was time to get it over with, you know? Things have been weird between us since that night at the lake, and I'm sick of it. I thought maybe if we slept together it would take the mystery and intrigue out of it all and we could go back to being friends...or whatever we were."

His blue eyes lasered into hers, and Cat felt compelled to say more.

"Plus, Lacey kind of dared me..." Jesus, on top of that being totally out of context, it sounded so frigging lame. "It felt like the thing to do at the time. Especially after a few drinks."

He cocked his head to the side, and let out a short laugh. "So you're telling me you were drunk? Because you seem pretty coherent now."

"At first I was," she amended flatly. But was that even the truth? From the second she'd gotten close enough to smell him, to feel the heat coming from his body, she'd been as sober as a funeral director. She could have changed her mind then, just as she'd almost done on the way up. But instinct and the need to get closer and explore the electricity arcing between them had overridden the warning bells jangling off in the distance the entire time.

"And then?" he pressed, unrelenting.

There was the question. The one she didn't want to answer—not out loud, anyway—and he saved her from having to.

"And then you did what you wanted, regardless of the consequences, just like you always do." His gaze was as intense as she'd ever seen it, and she shivered. "Are you happy now, Mary Catherine?"

Hell if that didn't make her sound like the spoiled little brat he'd called her back at the lake that night. But he didn't know the half of it. That it wasn't just his refusal that had haunted her. It was him. Everything about him. Exasperated, she ran a hand through her hair. "Look, I'm done discussing this. We did it. It's over and I, for one, would like to pretend it never happened."

"You can do that if you like." He rolled off the bed and padded toward her, completely unconcerned about his nakedness or the fact that, in spite of their recent activities, his body hadn't gotten the memo that they were done. "But I'll tell you one thing. I'm definitely not going to pretend it never happened. On the contrary, I'm going to think about it every day when I wake up, and every night when I go to sleep, and probably at various points in between."

He stopped two feet in front of her, and the breath froze in her throat as she craned her neck to look at him. God, he was gorgeous, and the gaze that had left her feeling so exposed only made her feel more so now. He brushed a curl back from her face with a gentle finger.

"Want to know something else?"

She shook her head no, but his lips tilted in a mocking smile and he continued anyway. "I'm going to put in some real thought about how to make *that*"—he tipped his head toward the bed—"happen again, real soon. Because in spite of your actions, you're grown now. It's open season, and you're fair game."

She swallowed hard and cleared her tight throat. "Yeah, well, don't hold your breath. I'm not interested. Besides, my brother loves you and all, but he won't like us being each other's booty call."

"Who said anything about booty calls? I can get laid anytime. I'm talking about me and you, together." He cupped her cheek and bent low toward her, until she could feel his warm breath on her lips.

Her eyes started to drift closed of their own volition, and his mouth brushed hers lightly as he spoke. "You liked what we did, didn't you, Mary Catherine?" His voice was low, hypnotic, and it made her insides quiver as surely as any touch.

"The way our bodies fit together, nice and tight." He closed his teeth over her bottom lip, and she whimpered. "The way my mouth felt on you. God, I can still taste it. So fucking good."

The groan sounded as if it was ripped out of him, and her nipples pebbled in response. The heat of his body called to her, overruling common sense. She leaned forward to press closer, to grind her hips to his and release the sudden tension building deep inside her, but he abruptly stepped back. Her eyes snapped open, and before she could formulate a response, he turned and headed toward the bed, the muscles in his back rolling and bunching with each step. She hesitated, still mesmerized, for a second too long and he turned back, catching her. "See something you like?"

She swallowed hard and wet her lips but couldn't conjure a response.

"If you changed your mind about running," he drawled, a challenging brow raised, "we can get right back into this bed. Or the shower. Or on that dresser, if you're feeling up to it."

Feeling up to it? What a joke. She was dying inside, and he didn't even know it. No one knew how she'd felt that night at the lake, not even Lacey. Hell, who was she kidding? Even with all her teenage fantasies, she couldn't have guessed how perfect their chemistry was going to be until she'd gone and opened up Pandora's box. And now it was too damned late to do anything about it.

She clutched the sheet tighter, twisting the linen as she stared at him, willing the voice of reason to scream with some advice she could use, but that fucker was as quiet as a laryngitis patient. She cleared her throat to say something, anything, but all that came out was air.

Was he grinning? Oh, hell no. He wasn't going to treat her like a child who amused him again. That thought straightened her spine, and she was grateful for the anger that quickly replaced her confusion. "Just so we're clear here. There is no me and you in that bed or shower or on the dresser even. We had sex. Period. Over. Done."

He hiked a dark brow at her, and she hiked one right back.

"Besides, it isn't like we'd make a good couple or something."

"You're right about that. I only have relationships with grown-ups," he said flatly, scooping his clothes off the floor. "Run away, little kitten. And don't be afraid, I'll be gone when you come out."

...

"You did what?" Lacey expressive face was lit up with an array of emotions ranging from shock to excitement.

They sat across from each other in Lacey's cozy, country-style kitchen and Cat debated exactly how much to tell her. They'd gotten back from Atlantic City the day before, and Cat had managed to put off spilling the story until now, with the excuse that Galen had been around every time she'd seen her. Now, with Galen out picking up the sandwiches for tonight's football game, it was just the two of them, and she hadn't been able to put it off any longer.

Cat slumped forward onto the smooth butcher-block island, cradled her head in her hands, and nodded. "Yes. Although 'slept with' is a misnomer. And worse? It was good."

"Boring, serious Shane, huh?"

"Do you have to sound so frigging giddy about it?" she groaned.

"Sorry. It's just...wait, so how come you're *not* giddy about it if it was so great?" Her excitement dimmed some and Cat felt a little better that she was taking this more seriously. Lacey pushed her stool away from the island and stood. "You still haven't told me how you guys left things or what you said to him afterward." She crossed the room to the refrigerator and pulled out Tupperware containers, setting them on the counter.

What *had* she said to him afterward? Not much, before she'd stomped off into the bathroom and he'd left. That still burned her ass. He'd tossed down the gauntlet, asking her if she was going to woman-up and work through what happened like an adult, or if she was going to run away and hide, and she'd done exactly that.

Wimp.

Now how was she supposed to save face, especially after his parting shot, when she'd behaved exactly like the child he'd accused her of being? That her actions were born of fear and self-preservation didn't absolve her. For a split second, she reconsidered committing to the whole drunk thing, but the thought shamed her before it was even fully formed. Making like some wilting daisy he'd taken advantage of somehow? That wasn't her. Sure, he could've spoken up, been the voice of reason, but he'd been asleep and all but molested. And he did try to stop at one point at the end. The fact that he'd given her what she'd begged for was hardly grounds for her disdain. There had to have been a time in there somewhere when they both could—and should—have stopped. But they'd willfully ignored it, the pleasure so keen, it clearly would have taken a person far stronger than either of them to manage it.

Explaining that to Lacey was going to be the dicey part. She'd already been nagging her lately about her commitment issues, and Cat knew if Lacey got wind of the fact that Shane had admitted to wanting more, she was going to get all up in her grill about fixing them up for real. Nothing would make her happier than to have them all settled in, right and tight, as a happy little foursome. Double dating, sharing recipes, making quilts…or worse, making babies. Together forever. And ever. And ever. Like her parents.

Ugh.

She loved them dearly, and while they both seemed content with their lot, her mother had given up a promising career as a concert violinist, moving from New York City to Rhode Island when Cat's father had been transferred. Once Galen was born, she'd made the decision to be a full-time mother and wife. At various points over the years, when times were lean, she'd made extra money teaching snobby fourth-graders their scales, but for the majority of Cat's life, her

Stradivarius had remained in its case on a shelf in the study, like a rectangular urn full of dreams turned to ash. Every so often, Cat would catch her mother standing in front of it, trailing a loving finger over the worn leather with a wistful smile.

Panic trickled down her neck, settling at the base of her spine like a parasite. She broke eye contact, instead focusing on the lemon-yellow walls of the kitchen. Odd how the color that usually cheered her made her want to hiss like a vampire faced with daylight. When she looked at Lacey again, her friend's arms were crossed as she waited for a response.

Time to bob and weave. "I, uh, I don't really think much was said afterward. Hell, I don't even know how it happened in the first place. Before I had a chance to second-guess myself, it was to the point of no return, if you know what I mean." She waggled her brows in a move meant to add levity as well as to fluster her reserved friend, but it didn't work. Lacey eyed her speculatively.

"So you mean to tell me, the first time you guys are together, and—by your own admission—within a very short period of time, there was a 'point of no return' for you? That's pretty spectacular out of him, no? Psychic high five to Shane." She swung her hand in the air to mimic the gesture and frowned. "So why do you look less than impressed?"

"Well, first off, we don't even like each other. I mean, he all but told me I was immature, and I flat-out told him he wasn't my type. I live life on the edge, I like spontaneity and fun. He likes…whatever the opposite of that is."

Lacey glared at her. "Does that description remind you of anyone else you know?"

Belatedly, Cat recalled that Lacey was made from a similar mold, and the two of them had been best friends since grade school in spite of the fact that they were polar opposites. "Yes, but at least you let me do me. He was like my self-appointed guard dog after Galen left. Do you know how many times he ruined my fun that year? I can't have someone thinking they're going to control me.

"Plus," Cat said, ticking off on her fingers as if there were so many things wrong with the idea of the two of them together, they required counting, "say things did get serious." *Never. Gonna. Happen.* "He lives halfway across the country. My job isn't something I can just up and leave. I've worked too hard to get where I am to walk away now. Not to mention, I've heard him say more than once that he wants a big family. I don't want babies at all. Talk about cramping my style," she added with a snort.

Lacey's tone went soft and wistful. "But they smell so good. That sweet baby scent. And those chubby little wrists and ankles." She turned to face Cat, eyes brimming with sudden, unshed tears. "I can't imagine not wanting one."

"Jesus, why are you crying? Did something happen?" Dread formed a knot in her stomach, and her own mini-drama took a backseat. She stood to take her friend's hand.

"No, no, I'm fine. It's just…" Lacey snuffled and shook her head with a watery grin. "It's so silly. We, ah, haven't exactly been trying, but we haven't been using any protection for the last few months since we both want to start a family soon. But nothing's happening and I'm afraid I'm—" She bit her lip and turned away.

"Hey, sweetie, stop that. Do you have any reason to believe that's the case? I mean, everything normal with your monthly and all? Have you been feeling okay?"

"Yes, it's just… We do it all the time. Like, a lot. Constantly. Your brother is very s—"

"Okay, I'm drawing a line in the sand. TMI. But I get it, you guys are active. Still, it takes a few months to get the Pill out of your system." She gave Lacey's arm a reassuring squeeze. "I'm sure it will be fine. If you want, make an appointment, and I'll go with you and hold your hand. Or an ankle, even, if need be."

This elicited the desired chuckle from her friend, and the tension in Cat's gut eased. "You were made for motherhood, Lace, and I have no doubt you'll be able to get pregnant. If something down the line makes that an issue, there are still so many options out there nowadays. I'll be crazy Auntie Cat before you know it, and I can't wait."

Lacey smiled and nodded. "I'm just being paranoid. I know you're right." A car door slammed, and she pulled away. "Galen must be back with the food." She swiped a hand over her eyes and blinked at Cat. "Is my mascara running?"

"Nope, all clear."

She jabbed a finger in Cat's face and frowned. "Do *not* think you're in the clear, sister. I'm not done with you by a long shot. We'll pick this Shane discussion up later."

Lacey made her way to the door to help Galen with the sandwiches and Cat let out a sigh of relief. Later was good. Later was a hundred times better than now. It would give her a chance to fine-tune her argument, and then Lacey wouldn't stand a chance. She'd spent a lifetime convincing her friend to see things her way. This would be no different.

If she could just avoid running into Shane over the next month, she'd be home free.

• • •

"Look who I found," Galen called down the long hallway.

Lacey threw her arms around Shane and squeezed. "Hey, you! I thought you were going over to your sister's tonight to see the twins?"

Shane shifted the bag of sandwiches to his other arm and hugged her back. "Abby has the stomach flu, so we had to postpone." He released her, and Galen ducked in to give his fiancée a quick kiss.

"Yeah, and I saw him at Sam's Subs getting a meatball grinder for the game, so I dragged him home with me. The only thing better than the Patriots beating the Giants is Shane being here when it happens."

Shane shook his head mournfully. "I feel sorry for you, man. And for you, Lace, having to live with this delusional bastard. The Pats are going down. The reaming Tom Brady is about to take from the Giants D is going to leave him sore for a week."

"Put your money where your mouth is, son."

Lacey rolled her eyes and smiled. "You two are ridiculous. Come on, let's get this stuff put out so we can eat." She took the bag from Shane and started down the photo-lined hallway. "Make sure you guys take your boots off if they're muddy and hang your coats in the closet," she called over her shoulder.

They complied before following her into the kitchen, where Cat stood at the island, laying out sandwich toppings. His pulse kicked up a notch when she turned to face him.

"Mary Catherine," he said with a nod, taking in her thunderous expression and full, glossy lips. In the past forty-eight hours, it had been his biggest regret that they hadn't really kissed that night in Atlantic City. Granted there were other—a million other—things he wanted to do with her…to her, that he hadn't had the chance to do, but the fact that he hadn't tasted those lips for real in almost ten years? It was a fucking crime, and he wouldn't let it stand. But she didn't need to know that. Not yet, at any rate.

"It's Cat. And I thought you weren't going to be here?"

She said it with a smile, but there was no mistaking the tightness in her voice. Lacey set the bag down and stepped between them, hands fluttering. "Abby is sick, so we're lucky to have Shane with us tonight. Isn't that great?"

The daggers those soft brown eyes were shooting at Cat

said it all. Lacey knew what had happened between them. Interesting. He'd wondered if Cat would keep it to herself and try to pretend it never happened, but apparently, she had been compelled to share it with her best friend. Maybe that was a good sign? Although judging by the way her arms were crossed over her chest and from the expression on her face, he was guessing not.

"Yeah. Great," Cat replied flatly. "Is the rest of the crew coming?"

"Rafe was supposed to come, but he got stuck at the precinct, and Mick is away on business, so it's just us. Mom and Dad might swing by for the second half, but that's about it."

"Lovely."

Clearly the idea of a foursome didn't sit well with her, but it was fine by him.

Galen set his bag down on the counter and frowned at his sister. "What crawled up your ass and died?"

Cat unfolded her arms and shook her head. "Nothing, I'm good. Just tired."

"Tired from what? Aren't you on vacation this week?" he asked.

She made a show of fussing with the napkins. "Yes, but I still got up early and went to the gym. Plus I had a lot of errands to run."

Shane took a closer look at her face and noted the dark smudges under her eyes. Not sleeping well. Good. That made two of them.

"Galen, can you help me put some of these snacks out in the living room?" Lacey asked loudly, leading the way from of the kitchen.

Galen's gaze flickered between his sister and Shane for a moment before he followed. "Sure. Right behind you."

Once Shane gauged that they were out of earshot, he

rounded the island to get closer to Cat, keeping his voice low. "Listen, I—"

She wheeled on him, quick as a snake. "No, you listen," she whispered, keeping an eye on the doorway behind him. "I like you, Shane. You're a good guy, and I don't want things to be weird between us, but I didn't expect to see you this soon after…the thing. So cut me some slack, would you? It was a mistake. I really don't know what I was thinking. The sooner we forget it, the quicker things can go back to normal. Let's just get through the next few weeks until you go back to California, and this will all be a nonissue."

The words weren't a surprise. Hell, he'd known she was going to do her best to shove it under the rug, but the knowing didn't make it sting any less. He curled his lips into what he hoped resembled a smile, trying to ignore the way her breasts heaved against the fitted green sweater she wore. "Take it easy there, killer. I was just going to ask you not to mention it to your brother. I know you told Lacey, but I think it would make things a little awkward trying to explain it to Galen. I don't think either one of us needs the hassle."

Cat cleared her throat and nodded. "Oh. Yeah, well, duh. I wasn't going to tell him." She unscrewed the cap of a pickle jar and laid the spears on a plate, unwilling to meet his gaze. "And I only told Lacey because she was suspicious that something was up. I'm not a good liar."

Could have fooled him. She was clearly a pro at lying to herself. "Well, I'll leave you to—" he tipped his chin toward the counter where she was building the leaning tower of pickles, way too high for the number of people there "—whatever it is you're doing. You coming soon, or you planning to avoid me for the next few hours?"

Ha. Judging by the look on her face, the next few *years* was probably more like it, but he wasn't going to let that happen. Before he'd left Cali, he'd already put in transfer paperwork in order to be closer to his family. He'd gotten the call this morning that everything was a go, and after tying up some loose ends later in the month, he'd be on the East Coast for good. And, for the foreseeable future, he had every intention of making sure he was front and center, in Cat's face, making it impossible to forget what they'd done together. For her to be as haunted by the memory as he was. The way she'd felt, body pressed against his, gasping and writhing. The way she'd broken apart in his arms and groaned his name. His cock swelled, straining against his zipper.

She gifted him with a tight smile. "Nope. No avoidance here. As long as you're going to be cool, I'm cool. It was just sex, after all, and we're both adults. No biggie."

Right. No biggie.

"Great." He edged around her, accidentally-on-purpose brushing his torso against hers when he passed, and she stiffened. "I'm going to grab a beer from the fridge, you want one?"

"No, thanks."

Her voice sounded a little huskier than it had a moment before, and he bit back a grin and helped himself to a lager. Flipping off the cap, he threw a lingering look over his shoulder, letting his gaze travel the length of her before he walked out. "By the way, you might want to turn the heat up in here. You look cold."

Chapter Four

Cat glared down at her traitorous nipples, clearly visible against the teal cashmere. At that moment, she couldn't determine whether it was the incidental contact or the earthy scent of his cologne that brought the memories rushing in, but damned if she didn't have the sudden urge to drag him back into the kitchen and see if the countertops were as sturdy as they looked.

But for him to call attention to it? What a bastard. And she was the one who needed to grow up?

"The game's starting," Galen called from the living room.

She straightened her shoulders, pasted a smile on her face, and scooped up a basket of chips and a bowl of dip. After a quick nipple check, she called back, "Coming!" and went to join them.

It took a couple hours, but eventually, she was actually able to enjoy herself. For the first half of the game, she'd been on edge, waiting for Shane to slip up about their indiscretion or embarrass her somehow. But aside from his comment in the kitchen, he'd acted like everything was normal. Maybe he really was going to let her off the hook *that* easily.

Once it was apparent he'd decided to behave, she settled in, allowing herself to relax and soak up the warmth of the crackling fire. That was nice. Galen never used to light it.

She peered around the room and noted that, in the past few months since she'd moved in, Lacey had really lent the place a warm touch all over. Cat had seen it at points, in transition, but seeing it all come together was something else. The soothing earth-toned walls and honey-colored hardwood floors made the living room feel like the welcoming great room at a ski lodge, compared with the almost sterile feel of the white walls and serviceable furniture Galen had preferred. It was nice and inviting. Still, she couldn't help but wonder if her brother liked the new look or if this was another one of those compromises that people in relationships did for their partner.

She was stretched out on the recliner in the corner, nursing her beer and contemplating that, when the smack talk got loud. This was the best part of football season, and she was as loud as the guys, name-calling and whooping it up. The Patriots were up by fourteen, and Galen had his sights set on Shane.

"I can already taste the lunch you're going to have to buy me tomorrow when the Pats log this win. But, man, don't feel bad. There's always next week. And Eli's such a good quarterback. Did you know, he's the third-most-famous quarterback..."

"...in his family," Cat deadpanned, as was expected of her. Her brother stuck his hand behind him from his perch on the beanbag chair in front of her for a low five, and she complied with a laugh.

"Say what you want, but he's a come-from-behind kind of guy," Shane said, from his seat on the couch next to Lacey, eyes glued to the set. "Anything can happen."

"There you, go, Shane. That's some team spirit," Lacey said. She didn't really care for football much, but she tended to join in on the jabber anyway, and always in support of the underdog. Another reason Cat loved her so much.

"I don't know. He's doing a lot of scrambling in the pocket. Maybe your O-line should start thinking about waking up and buying him some time?" Galen piped in.

Shane tipped his head and shrugged. "If a guy really knows what he's doing, he doesn't need a lot of time." Was it her imagination, or had his voice gotten deeper? "He makes the most of the time he's given."

Galen spouted off about benefits and detriments of a quick-fire quarterback, but Cat stayed silent, suspicious eyes on Shane. He took a pull from his beer, his gaze still locked on the TV, in spite of the commercial break. A long moment later, she finally decided that he was actually talking football and not baiting her with sexual innuendos as she'd suspected. Until he winked. Or blinked? She was directly to his left, so she could only see his one eye. Son of a bitch, he was driving her nuts.

She popped a handful of cashews in her mouth and crunched them harder than necessary.

"Anyway," Galen continued, "I think it's good to have more than one secret weapon in your arsenal, you know. And speaking of secrets. Shane." The intensity of her brother's expression belied his casual tone. "Got anything you want to tell me?"

Terror hit harder than Holyfield, and Cat sucked in a panicked breath. Along with it came a wayward cashew, which lodged itself neatly in her windpipe. A little nugget of doom. Her mind reeled, the fear of being found out oddly no less potent for a moment than the fear of choking to death, and how sad was that? She tried to cough, but nothing happened. And that's when it really hit her. She was actually in trouble here. She clutched at her throat, Shane's voice dimly penetrating the sound of blood pounding in her ears.

"What do you mean, bro?"

They had no idea. She was dying and they had no clue. She wanted to scream, but no sound would come. Instead, she shot up, waving her arms, frantically pointing to her neck.

"Cat! Oh my God, she's choking!" Lacey screamed.

Shane was on his feet in an instant and behind her in less, with his firm thigh planted between her legs. His strong arms wrapped around her without hesitation, his cupped fist just above her belly.

"It's going to be okay," he murmured, his voice almost unnaturally calm. "Ready? Here we go." He thrust up and in once, hard, sending the cashew along with some other nutty shrapnel flying out of out of her mouth at breakneck speeds.

She gulped at the air, desperate for oxygen like she'd never known it, despite having only been without for a short time. She'd held her breath under water far longer, but the forced deprivation had made even these twenty seconds feel like an eternity.

"Are you okay? Should we call 911?" Galen asked, his eyes on Shane.

"I don't think that's necessary. Give her a minute, and I think she'll be fine." Shane turned her to face him, his perceptive eyes searching her face. "You good?"

She nodded, swiping a trembling hand over her mouth. "Scared the shit out of me, but I'm okay."

The eerie calm seemed to falter as fear flickered in his eyes and his jaw tensed. "Maybe try chewing those next time."

Charming. Before she could shoot off a response, Lacey had grabbed her and was shaking her by the shoulders. "Oh my God, Cat. That was awful. Are you sure you shouldn't go to the ER?"

Cat managed a weak laugh and shook her head. "I'm just

a little freaked out. Let me sit for a minute and I'll be like new."

She sank back into the recliner and closed her eyes for a second. Shane was right. Aside from the jittery adrenaline dump and a bit of an ache where Shane had Heimlich-ed her, she felt like nothing had happened. She tuned back into the conversation and caught the tail end of Lacey and Galen praising Shane on his quick response. She hadn't even thanked him.

"You were great," Cat chimed in. "Thanks for...uh..." *What? Saving my ass? Bailing me out of trouble, just like old times?* Instead she waved her hands around in the general direction of where they'd been standing, "You know, *that*. I really appreciate it."

"I'm just glad you're okay."

Lacey insisted on getting Cat a bottle of water and taking the cashews from her, which was fine by Cat. Cashews were officially right up there with sushi and liver now. Never to pass her lips again.

A few minutes later, everyone had settled back in and Cat's hopes for a reprieve started to build when Galen turned to Shane.

"So before Cat decided to steal your thunder, you were about to tell us something."

It wasn't a question.

Cat's throat closed up again, but this time there was no nut to blame. She pinched the bridge of her nose between her finger and thumb and let out a sigh. "Look, this isn't really anyone else's business. We—"

"I guess you heard it from my mother, then?" Shane cut in smoothly, attention still locked on Galen.

Jesus Christ on a stick, he told his mom? That was just wrong. "Listen, I—"

"It wasn't official until today," Shane continued, sending

her a quick, pointed glance, "but I guess I should've known the second I let the town crier in on it, word would get out. I put in a transfer request last month and it was approved. So, you heard right. I'm moving."

For the second time in the past hour, Cat nearly wept with relief. So Galen didn't know about her and Shane. She took a steadying breath and stepped away from the mental ledge. Shane's mother was a love, but she did have an ear—and mouth—for gossip. Not the venomous kind, but she always seemed to be the first to know if someone's kid was going to medical school or about a new beau.

"Where you headed?" Cat waited, the curiosity making her stomach dip, and not in a pleasant way. When he'd been on the West Coast, it had been perfect because it made anything more than an annual trip difficult. Still, as long as he wasn't too close, she'd manage. She even conjured up an interested smile for him.

"Headed?" Galen said, a huge grin splitting his face. "He's not headed anywhere. He's coming home."

Cat's stomach nose-dived, landing somewhere in the vicinity of her feet, and her head began to swim. Shane. Home for good. What had she done to deserve this?

"How exciting!" Lacey squealed and leapt to her feet. "This calls for a celebration."

"It's going to be great to have you back," Galen said.

Cat barely registered the hubbub over Shane's imminent return because for her, it meant nothing but trouble...

Run away, kitten.

"To Shane." Lacey said, holding up her pint glass.

Cat's hand shook as she held up her water bottle to join the toast. She could feel Lacey's gaze drilling into her. She'd given her friend a pile of excuses for why she shouldn't date Shane and already the whole long-distance one was shot to hell. If the rest didn't hold, soon she would be faced with a very unpleasant truth. A truth she wasn't about to trot out for show-and-tell right now because it had already been a long and confusing couple of days. She chugged the rest of her water and set the bottle on the table.

"Anyone need anything while I'm up?" Galen asked, heading for the kitchen.

"I'll take a Winterfest, if you're buying," Shane said.

Mind still reeling, Cat was tempted to add a snifter of cyanide to the list of requested refreshments when Lacey pointed to the TV. "Oh, that's the site Rafe just joined."

Rafe was a longtime friend. He and Galen had boxed together in high school, and they'd been tight ever since. Shorter and leaner than Galen, he'd been a middleweight, fast as lightning, but not quite crisp enough to make a living at it. He'd moved on to MMA and was still fighting semipro, but he was also a detective in the Crimes Against Persons Unit at the Wesley Police Department.

Cat turned her attention to the advertisement for a dating site, featuring several satisfied customers extolling the virtues of finding love online.

"Fun, right? Rafe said that when he gets some hits, he's going to have me come over and help him pick his dates." Lacey waggled her brows suggestively. "I think online dating seems like a great way to meet people. Especially for someone as busy as Rafe." She turned to face Shane, eyeing him speculatively. "Hey, you're coming home soon. You should join, too."

Wait, did that mean she was going to get off her jock about this Shane thing, or was Little Miss Innocent trying to be slick somehow? Cat eyed her friend hard but saw nothing but sincerity shining back. Okay, so maybe she really was trying to help. Finding Shane the kind of girl who wanted to settle down would be awesome. Maybe then he wouldn't be such a temptation.

"I think it's a great idea," Cat said, with what she hoped passed for an encouraging grin.

Shane met her gaze, eyes glittering with something that had her cheeks going all hot. "Do you?" he asked softly.

She took a gulp from the dregs of her warm, pre-choking beer and swallowed hard before responding. "I do. And you've been gone so long, it will get you meeting some new people in the area and whatnot. Plus, if your quarterback can't score, at least maybe you'll get a chance to."

Galen let out a low whistle. "Dang, them's fighting words."

When Shane's lips split into a challenging smile, a shiver went through her. "You're very confident for only being up seven points. Care to make a wager?" he asked.

She didn't answer right away, a sudden, jittery feeling making it hard to resist the urge to see if her nostrils were quivering like a bunny downwind of a fox.

"What's the matter? You don't have faith in your team? Up by seven and there's less than four minutes to go. Either you believe in your team and will make a wager, or you won't."

Lacey and Galen were hanging on their every word now, wanting to get in on the fun. Far be it from her to disappoint them or back down. He'd run her off earlier that weekend, and she wasn't about to let it happen twice. She was nobody's chicken.

"Bet your ass I will. Let's hear it."

"If the Pats win, I'll join your dating site. If they lose," his voice dropped, and his eyes went dark, "*you* go on a date with me."

Either the room went silent or the blood suddenly buzzing in her ears had rendered her deaf, because for a few seconds, she couldn't hear shit. She *could* feel the weight of everyone's eyes on her, though. She shifted in her seat, and opened and closed her mouth wordlessly. What the hell was going on here? One minute he was acting like he was cool with them keeping everything on the down low and moving on like it never happened, the next he was asking her out in front of everyone.

"A date? What kind of date?" Galen asked, but they were saved from answering when Lacey elbowed him in the stomach.

"Shh, mind your own business. This is getting interesting."

Cat ignored them, wholly focused on Shane now. "How do I know you'll go out with anyone? Just joining the site isn't really a big deal. Anyone can do that part."

He shrugged. "You can do for me what Rafe is letting Lacey do for him. Help me choose. Be my wingman, so to speak."

"Seriously?"

Shane didn't answer. Instead he kept his intense gaze trained on her. Clearly, he was dead serious. Everyone knew she was reckless, and backing away from a challenge went against the grain. The longer she stalled, the more awkward this was going to get.

And the more obvious that something deeper was at play here.

"Fine. Whatever." She shrugged and swiped at some imaginary crumbs on her sweater. "On the off chance that the Pats blow this game, I guess I can stay awake through a meal with you. But you have to promise to go on at least five dates if you lose. If you're not going to give it a real chance, it's not worth it."

"Done."

With the bet set, everyone turned attention back to the game, although she could sense Galen's sidelong glances flicking between her and Shane. No time to worry about it now, though. The Giants were marching steadily down the field, and Cat watched the action with bated breath, noting that everyone else seemed just as invested. Even Galen was up and pacing, and Lacey had taken to covering her eyes during key plays. Cat turned her attention back to the TV set just in time to see Eli flat on his back. Again.

It was looking good for her and the Pats. Soon, she'd get to help find Shane a girlfriend. Hell, he could be happy and settled by spring.

Exactly what she'd wanted, right?

So why did the prospect of winning the bet suddenly feel a little like losing?

...

Shane sat back and watched the rest of the game, entirely unconcerned about the outcome.

Of concern, though, were the dark, searching looks Galen was giving him. The opportunity had opened up and he'd taken it, but he'd also given his buddy a bead on his feelings for Cat, and he needed to prepare himself for the confrontation. If he knew his friend the way he thought he did, once Galen realized that he was as serious as a terrorist threat about his sister, he'd be okay with it. Cat's carousel of a love life had been tough for her big brother to watch, and as long as he knew Shane wasn't just trying to hop on for a quick ride, he'd give his blessing.

If only convincing Cat would be that easy.

She was a tough one. Although right now, she was looking anything but tough. She was a wreck. The Giants were at fourth and goal, and if they made it into the end zone, the game would go into overtime, giving them a chance to win.

A minute later, the room erupted into boos and cheers simultaneously when Eli threw an incomplete pass, locking up the win for the Patriots and for Cat. He tried not to let her whooping and whistling bruise his ego.

"All right, there we go. That's what I'm talking about.

Ladies and gents, introduce yourself to the newest member of MeetMyMate.com." She waved a flourishing hand toward Shane. "And don't worry, I'll make sure we clean him up before we put up his video. This is going to be fun."

He sure thought so, which was odd, because if someone had asked him an hour ago if he'd rather swim with sharks or join an online dating site, Jaws would have won, hands down. Now that he'd gotten a second taste of Cat, nothing was going to stop him from getting more.

The women were chattering about his hair and what kinds of things he should say in his introduction video when he noticed Galen standing in the kitchen doorway, giving him the hairy eyeball. He jerked his head to the side, a clear invitation to join him on the down low.

"I'm going to get a sandwich," he announced, but neither of them paid him any mind.

When he stepped through the doorway, Galen was leaning against the counter, arms akimbo. "So what's the deal, man? Got something you want to tell me?"

Shane weighed his options and decided to shoot from the hip. "Yeah, I guess I do. I'm into Cat. Have been for years, but never felt like the time was right or that she was ready to hear it. I want to be closer to friends and family, but I'm not going to lie. Part of the reason I decided to come back was to see if she was ready."

The tension in Galen's jaw dissipated and he nodded slowly. "Okay. So what's the plan?"

"She definitely has some feelings for me. I think she's going to need a little convincing to see things my way, but only because she's Cat." Shane crossed his arms over his chest. "Is this all going to be a problem for you?"

Galen rubbed at his chin and then shook his head. "Not when you put it like that, I guess. But why didn't you tell me before?"

"You mean like when you asked me to take care of her while you went to college, and open a can of whoop-ass on any guy who touched her? Or do you mean during those long heart-to-hearts we used to have at sleepovers right before we did our nails and had a pillow fight? Come on, buddy. We've gone out drinking, took a couple trips, kayaked, played racquetball, hell, even sparred together, but we don't do a whole lot of deep-feeling swaps. Do you remember how you told me that you and Lacey were together?"

Galen shrugged a beefy shoulder. "Not exactly."

"You called me up and said, 'Hey, me and Lacey are getting married but we haven't nailed down the date yet.' Before that, I hadn't heard shit about you two. I didn't say anything about Cat because there was nothing to tell. Now there is."

His friend snorted and grinned. "I guess. Okay, so what now? Why the dating site? Now she's going to be focused on hooking you up with other chicks. Seems ass-backward."

"I'll get to spend a lot of alone time with her. Not to mention, she's going to be shining me up some, putting my best foot forward, so to speak. Maybe she'll find she doesn't much like the idea of having to send me out into the world of adoring females."

Galen cracked out a laugh and pushed off the counter. "Good luck with that, man. You're going to need it. If she's got her mind made up, it'll take hell freezing over to change it." He clapped Shane on the shoulder as he passed on his way back to the living room. "On the real, though? There's no one I'd rather see her with. You're my brother already, but it'd be nice to make it legit."

Shane stayed in the kitchen a minute longer, sawing off a hunk of sandwich he didn't want and slapping it on a paper plate. Galen's blessing had lifted that last bit of weight off his chest, leaving him free to do whatever he had to do to get Cat to wake the fuck up and see what was right in front of her. His friend had been dead-on in one respect, though. The thing with a bullheaded woman like Cat was to make her think it was her idea. Best way to do that? Stick with the plan, and let her do the chasing.

He scooped up his plate and a bottled water and was about to join the group when Cat came barreling in, coat in hand.

"If you're going to drive me then let's go." She tapped an exasperated toe on the tile floor.

"What are you talking about?"

"Lacey and I went shopping earlier and came straight back here, so I don't have my car. Galen was going to take me home, but he said he's had too much to drink and that you were taking me."

"Ah, okay. Let me just say my goodbyes and stick this in a to-go bag."

The toe percussion slowed to a waltz tempo and her annoyed expression faltered. "Did he not even ask you?"

"He didn't mention it, no, but it's not a problem. I go right by your place."

Her eyes narrowed. "I thought you put him up to it."

"Nope. I would have liked to give it a shot between us, but you clearly have your mind made up, so why waste my time? Come on, I'll drop you home and we can talk about when we should get together to do this dating site thing. I'm hot to get started."

He was hot all right. Probably from his pants being on fire after that laundry list of lies he'd just fed her. He refused to feel guilty, though. He was going to wring every last drop out of their time together and hope that deep down she wanted him enough to find she hated the idea of him with someone else.

She seemed to accept what he said at face value and waited by the door while he said his good-byes. A few minutes later, they were in his rental truck and pulling out of the driveway.

"It's supposed to snow day after tomorrow," she said, tracing the icy condensation on the passenger window with a gloved fingertip.

"Yeah, I heard that. Glad I bought my parents that snowblower last year. I'll be able to clear it out quick. Being stuck inside makes me feel caged."

"Me, too. That's the worst. Especially on vacation days. I've got some things planned that I have to cross off my list, but I may have to fit in a skiing day, too, if it's looking good out there."

"Still working off that list, huh?"

The question hung heavy between them, and he wondered if she remembered the night she'd told him about her bucket list as vividly as he did.

It was a Saturday in September. The Indian summer had gifted them with a balmy night, and everyone was hanging by the bonfire in the backyard of Bobby Boyd's lake house.

Everyone except for Cat.

One minute she was there, the next she was gone. He'd searched the yard for her, then the house, but no luck. He had just started getting worried when he saw Lacey peering toward the lake while chewing her bottom lip.

"Spill it, munchkin," he demanded.

She looked up in his general direction but wouldn't meet his gaze. "Spill what?"

He sighed and ran a hand through his hair, looking down toward the lake. "Is she with a guy or alone?" He wasn't sure which answer he wanted to hear at that moment. Both sucked.

Lacey swallowed hard and leaned in to whisper. "Alone. But she told me not to tell you where she was. It's just, she's been gone a while and I'm getting nervous."

Nervousness was an almost perpetual state for Lacey, so that in itself wasn't cause for concern, but a young woman in the lake at night was. She could swim out too far and get a cramp, or some asshole could take her solitude as an invitation. "I'm going to check on her. And don't worry. I won't tell her you said anything."

When he'd finally made his way to the spit of beach down the path, it was to find her standing ankle-deep in the water, wearing only her bra and underwear. He'd nearly swallowed his tongue.

"Figures. Lacey Drawers couldn't keep her trap shut, huh?" She didn't sound mad. More teasing than anything. "I told her if she was so worried, she should come with me, but that didn't work. She said we could skinny-dip next time we go to our lake cottage, but really, when are we ever left alone long enough to do that?" She turned to face him, full on in the buttery moonlight, and the breath stuck in his chest. "Still, the water looks almost black, and my imagination started running away with me."

He finally peeled the tongue from the roof of his mouth to speak. "You shouldn't be here by yourself, Mary Catherine. It's dangerous."

"Well, it would seem I'm not by myself after all, wouldn't it now, Decker?" She gave him the smile that never ceased to make his gut ache and started forward into the water.

He stepped in after her without hesitation, warm water lapping at his ankles and filling his sneakers.

"Don't."

"I've got to." She shrugged her bare, white shoulders. "It's on my bucket list."

"What bucket list?" He asked, tearing his gaze from her satin-covered breasts. "That's for old people."

"It's for people who have things they want to make sure to experience before they die, and I've got a long one."

She hadn't stopped moving and was ten feet out now, up to her hips. He bit back a curse. "And let me guess, annoying the shit out of your brother's best friend is number one?"

Even then, she'd seen it. Known that annoyance was the least of the things he felt for her, at least that night. Her slow smile sent hormones screeching through his veins like a crazed banshee.

A low cough from the passenger's seat jarred him back to the present. He snuck a look to his right to see Cat toying with the belt of her coat. "Uh, yeah. Still working my way through the bucket list, albeit with some adjustments. I crossed out 'marry Justin Timberlake' and changed it to 'Ryan Gosling.' And erased 'move to Turkey and buy a monkey' altogether. You know, stuff like that."

Her voice was strained, so he opted to go along and play it light.

"Good call. I think he's married now anyway, and I hear monkeys are a pain in the ass. I hate to take up too much of your vacation, though, if you had plans. Are you sure you'll have time to do this dating site thing for me?"

"No, no. I want to!" Her rushed reassurance might have bruised his ego if it didn't seem so over the top. "And most of my plans are later in the week. Tomorrow and the next day are unwinding days. I just finished designing a collection and need to decompress before I start the next one. You free late tomorrow afternoon? I can come by your parents' house."

His lips quirked at the words she didn't say, but he heard loud and clear. *You know, your parents' house. Where your parents are and we won't have to be alone.*

Good. Making her nervous was very, very good.

"Sure, sounds perfect. Don't eat. You know my mom loves to feed people."

She adjusted her seat and seemed to settle in more comfortably. "Score. I love a free, mom-cooked meal."

The hum of the heater was the only noise for the rest of the five-minute drive, but the silence was more companionable.

He imagined she was pleased with how things were shaping up and was busy mentally dressing him for tomorrow's photo shoot. Which was sort of ironic, since he was pretty fucking satisfied with the way things were going, too, and mentally *un*dressing her.

The short leather coat she wore belted at the waist accentuated the fact that she was stacked both in the front and in the back, and he allowed himself to imagine that she wore nothing but the coat and those boots for him. That if he leaned over and tugged that leather bow, she would be unwrapped. An early birthday present. The sides of her coat would fall open—along with those creamy white thighs—and he'd have an unobstructed view of the sweet, round tits that he'd gotten to touch but not see. He'd—

"Slow down, my turn's next, remember?" she said, giving his arm a tap and jarring him back to reality. "Jeez, you've been away so long you don't remember where I live?"

"Sorry, I was daydreaming." And that little fantasy was costing him. He shifted in his seat in an effort to ease the pressure his jeans were exerting on the mother of all boners. One thing was for sure, there was no way he was getting a wink of sleep tonight unless he jerked off. *Man's gotta do what a man's gotta do.*

When they pulled up to Cat's tiny ranch a minute later, she turned to him. "Thanks a lot for the ride…and also for the whole Heimlich thing. It could've been really bad. I'm really glad you were there."

He didn't meet her gaze, sure the truth was plain on his face. That had scared the shit out of him. "Yeah, me, too. Come on, let's get you inside," he said, swinging open his door.

"Oh, Shane, you don't need to walk me up," she called after him when he stepped out of the car.

"It's late and dark and the ground's covered in ice. You didn't even leave your light on. Just come on."

She got out, and he rounded the car to her side, slamming the door behind her. It got him close enough to smell the citrus in her hair, which had his already-primed body tightening even further.

They walked side-by-side up the narrow walkway, arms brushing with each step. When they got to her porch he stopped at the bottom of the stairs. "Try to get some sleep. You look tired."

"Want me full of energy so I can pimp you right tomorrow, huh?" she said with a tight smile.

He nodded. "Something like that."

She started up the stairs and he turned to go, but a muffled oath had him whipping back around just in time to see her scrabbling for the railing. Too late. Her feet flew out from under her, and she went down like a bag of rocks. He managed to catch her from behind around the waist and stop her from hitting her chin on the concrete, but barely.

She hissed in a breath then exhaled a "Motherfucker!"

His heart thudded in his chest, and he lifted her gently to her feet, taking the brunt of her weight. "Did you break anything?"

She peered down in the moonlight with a mournful nod. "My Seven jeans."

Blood welled up under a jagged tear just above the knee, and he wanted to shake her. "Who cares about the jeans. Does anything hurt?"

"My wallet's going to hurt when I have to replace those jeans," she quipped weakly. She was playing the tough guy, but there was no mistaking the wince on her pale face when she pulled away from his grasp and tried to stand on her own.

"Shit, I'm so sorry, Cat. Lot of good I did, walking you up and then letting you fall down the stairs."

"It wasn't your fault. I was bound and determined to go down, I guess. I'm just glad you caught me and saved my teeth. That could've been really ugly."

He held her arm, leading her the rest of the way up. "Do you have any rock salt to melt the ice? Wouldn't want you falling down the steps again in the morning."

"I don't think so." She held out her hands and frowned at her torn gloves. "Guess it's a good thing I had these on, too."

"Yeah, it's your lucky day, and it's about to get even better. I'm coming inside, and you're getting at least half-naked so I can see that knee."

She paused, hand on the doorknob, to glare at him. "Why do you need to see it? I'm a grown woman and more than capable of taking care of it myself."

"You're going to let me look at that knee, or I'm going to bend you over mine."

The thought came with a mental snapshot that momentarily derailed his altruism, but he managed to tamp it down fast. She still stared up at him suspiciously.

"Cat, you're being ridiculous. I'm pretty sure I can handle the sight of you in your underwear without losing my shit."

Lie. He wasn't sure of that at all, but he needed to see that she took care of that cut, and he wasn't about to let her stop him. "I want to clean it so I can get a good look. See if you need stitches. Your brother would deck me if I left you like this and you got lockjaw or something. Although you unable to jabber might not be so terrible," he added just loud enough for her to hear.

She scowled at him but opened the door. "Fine. But I'm telling you right now, I'm not going to the ER for a tetanus shot no matter what. I hate them. They hurt for like a month," she said with a sniff and stepped into the foyer.

He sincerely hoped she didn't need one, since throwing her over his shoulder and dragging her to the ER could seriously hurt his chances of seeing her naked anytime soon. He said a silent prayer to the wound gods and followed her inside.

Chapter Five

Well, this is a grim way to end the evening, Cat thought bitterly. The scrape on her leg was stinging like the blazes, but her injured pride stung worse. Two times in one night, she'd managed to both humiliate herself and require rescuing. She may have mentally relegated him to the friend zone, but the rest of her hadn't gotten the memo, and she was fairly mortified at having horked up nut-chunks and taken a dive down the stairs in front of him. That her favorite jeans had succumbed during battle only made it worse.

Now, she sat on her toilet seat in bedtime boxers and a sweatshirt while Shane squatted in front of her, rubbing what felt like acid-treated shards of glass into her wound. "Shit, ouch!" She tried to pull away, but he had a firm grasp on her calf, pinning her in place.

"Stop moving." His tone was clipped and commanding. She wondered if that worked on the people he usually rescued because it wasn't doing shit for her.

"Stop torturing me, and I'll stop moving," she said through clenched teeth, gripping the sides of the bowl tighter when he only increased his efforts. "Seriously, is this fucking necessary? My butcher has gentler hands."

"Your butcher handles dead meat, so he can afford to be gentle. I'm trying to get the grime out of this scrape so it doesn't get infected. Now will you shut up for a second and let me concentrate?"

She bit her lip and turned her head when hot tears sprang to her eyes. What was she crying about? She'd had stitches a half dozen times in her life, not to mention the two broken bones she'd earned on the roller derby track a few years back. This injury was nothing in the scheme of things. But for some reason—maybe lack of sleep, maybe excess of Shane, maybe both—her emotions were bubbling up like cheese under a broiler.

"Almost done." He swiped some clear goop on it and sat back on his heels. "Looks like a pretty deep cut in the center there, but with the scrape surrounding it, stitches would be really uncomfortable. The bleeding's slowed a lot, so I don't think that's necessary. Let's bandage it tight and then when you come over tomorrow, we'll take another look, okay? As long as we keep it clean and covered until it starts to heal, I think it will be fine." His eyes met her in a frank stare. "You're going to have a scar, though."

She released her death grip on the porcelain. "That's okay, I have several. Beats having to go to the hospital."

"When was your last tetanus shot?"

"Three years ago. Cut my foot open on a rusty chunk of rudder in Montauk when I was surfing."

"That works. They're good for ten years for this type of thing." He stood and tossed the dirty Q-tips he'd been using into the trash can and set the antibacterial cream on the sink. "You going to bed soon or what?"

"As soon you leave. I'm exhausted, and I think the combination of choking and then falling shook me a little.

Why?" She eyed him warily, not sure where he was headed but pretty sure she wasn't going to like it.

"I want to bandage this in a way that allows you to sleep how you're used to. Part of the scrape is on your knee and anytime a cut is on a joint, keeping it covered is going to be a pain in the ass." He scooped up the roll of gauze and tape and held out a hand to her. "Come on. Let's get you into bed and you can show me how you lie."

She stared up at him, a flash of the last time they'd been near a bed together racing through her mind like a Cinemax flick. "Uh, that's okay. I sleep flat on my back, legs straight."

"For real?"

No. Not for real. But she had no intention of getting in bed with him nearby. She nodded vigorously, ignoring his outstretched hand and pushing herself to her feet with a wince.

"That's creepy. Do you fold your hands over your chest like a corpse?"

"No. But I do sleep in a coffin," she deadpanned, skirting around him for the door. "We can do the bandage in the living room. I'll get some scissors."

To her relief, he followed without any argument. She made her way gingerly to the kitchen, grabbed some scissors from a drawer, then settled onto the sprawling velvet couch with her leg outstretched. "Do your worst," she muttered, and pinched her eyes closed.

"Stop being a drama queen. This part shouldn't hurt."

He couldn't have been more wrong. It was killing her already, and he hadn't even touched her yet. Now, without the promise of pain to distract her, the thought of his hands all over her legs sent a shiver through her, and she gritted her teeth to suppress it. It was a no-go and she could feel the goose bumps breaking out on her skin.

"Want me to turn on the fireplace?" Shane asked. His

voice was coming from her feet now, where he was likely kneeling as he'd been in the bathroom. Semi-hysterical laughter bubbled as "while you're down there" jokes ran through her mind, unfiltered. She didn't trust her voice to answer him, so she just shook her head, resolutely keeping her eyes closed.

The whir of the tape and snip of the scissors seemed to echo through the quiet room, and she wished she'd turned on the TV. It felt like forever before he started the actual bandaging, but when he finally did, the reality was far worse than she'd even anticipated. The hand he used to steady her leg while he worked was big, hard, and intimate. And every time she thought he was done, he came back to adjust, add more tape...more touching. She wanted to look down so bad. To see if the calloused pads of his fingertips were absently caressing the soft skin on her inner thigh, or if she was imagining it. Either way, another rush of chills ran over her, and the breath caught in her throat.

"Cat?"

Shane's voice was low and husky...strained. Her eyes snapped open, and she stared into his. The look she found there sent her senses reeling. Stark, unapologetic need. The tension poured off him, and he leaned forward until their faces were only a few inches apart.

"Why are you afraid of me?"

"I'm n-not."

"Then why wouldn't you let me into your bedroom?"

"There was no need. I told you, I sleep flat on m—"

"Bullshit." He reached out a finger and trailed it over her cheekbone. "I spent a large chunk of my teen years at your house. You don't think I walked by your room sometimes and saw you sleeping like some ginger chinchilla, all rolled up in a ball?"

She drew back, his touch and that honeyed tone luring

her toward a place she didn't want to go. "Then why did you need to see if you already knew?"

"I wanted to lay the bandage on and see if it would be an issue. But don't try to deflect. Why the lie?" He closed the gap between them, his breath feathering her lips. "And why the goose bumps?" The fingers on her thigh tightened and suddenly, every good reason she'd come up with not to kiss him died.

She let herself lean in that last scant inch, and his warm lips covered hers. She didn't know what she'd expected, but the sweet rush of emotion clogging her throat wasn't it. His smell felt as familiar as the sunrise, and she instinctively leaned into him, taking the kiss deeper. She traced the seam of his mouth with the tip of her tongue, and he opened with a groan to meet it with his.

He rose up higher onto his knees and pushed her back into the cushions, slanting his torso over hers, taking control of the kiss, hot and demanding. He ran his tongue over the tender inside of her bottom lip, then sucked, sending a shiver of need through her. Her nipples stiffened and she plunged her fingers into his hair, wanting more, needing more.

Their harsh breathing was as sexy as any soundtrack she'd ever heard, and the rise and fall of his chest against her breasts slowly drove her insane. The skillful fingers that had been tracing circles on her thighs tightened, and he growled against her mouth. "I want you so bad," he gasped, pulling away to trail kisses over her jaw, along the length of her collarbone, heading for her breasts, which strained against her T-shirt, aching for his touch.

She froze, breath suspended, as he paused and then closed his teeth gently over her hard nipple through the thin cloth. She jerked forward as the touch blazed a path from her breast to her core. Moisture flooded between her thighs and she swallowed a cry.

Music sounded in the distance, and they both froze. He sent her a pained expression. "ABBA?"

It was. "Fernando," to be exact. Ever since Lacey had seen *Mamma Mia* on Broadway, she'd obsessed. *Saved by the ringtone.* "Yeah. That's Lacey calling. If I don't call her back, she'll be worried about me." Her heart was pounding so loud, it was a wonder she'd heard the phone at all, but thank God she had. She'd almost repeated the same foolish mistake.

He held her gaze for a long moment, then nodded. "Yeah." A muscle worked in his throat, but he released her instantly and stood. "And sorry about that. I shouldn't have let you kiss me. You're obviously having a rough day. Probably best if we forget it happened."

Forget it? Not bloody likely, but nice to know that he wanted to. Wait… "I kissed you? *You* kissed *me*." Even as she said it, the memory of his face inches in front of her before she dove at him like a seagull on a french fry ran through her mind. Jesus, she *had* kissed him.

He'd already grabbed his coat from the closet doorknob by the time she'd gathered her wits enough to respond, but he beat her to the punch.

"Sure. At least I was awake this time, right?" He pulled the coat over his broad shoulders and gave her a wink. "Take two ibuprofen before you go to sleep. You might be a little sore tomorrow." With that, he turned and walked out.

Son of a bitch. She stared at the closed door, baffled. How did she keep getting herself into these situations with him?

She snatched up her phone to whip off a text to Lacey, letting her know that she was home and exhausted, and that she would call her tomorrow. Then she put it on silent mode. She just didn't have the energy to talk about this shit right now.

With a sigh, she uncapped the pill bottle Shane had set on the table and tapped two orange tablets into her palm.

He'd given her the perfect excuse to cancel their appointment tomorrow. She could be sore and it would be so easy to take that lifeline, but then what? Avoiding him altogether was out of the question now that he'd be home for good soon. Not to mention she'd never backed out on a bet.

Hell, who was she kidding? There was way more at stake here than either of those things. After their near miss, it had become crystal clear—if she didn't get Shane settled down with a nice girl soon, she might not be able to resist the temptation to fill the slot herself. Not okay, since "settled down" and "nice girl" were so not on her bucket list.

Decision made, she popped the pills into her mouth, washing them down with a gulp of ice-cold water. Time to break those newly forming ties to Shane before she was bound and tied forever.

Chapter Six

The doorbell rang and Shane crossed the room to answer it. Cat stood on the porch wrapped in a long, wool coat. There was no reason to think she'd be naked underneath, but his dick was clearly more optimistic. He had to cut the big guy some slack, though. It had been a restless night for both of them, and he'd been tortured by the most erotic dreams he'd ever had after his kiss with Cat. He'd been so right about that. Now that he'd tasted those lips again, they were all he could think about.

He pulled himself together quickly and opened his mouth to greet her, but she cut in before he had the chance.

"Are your mom and dad home?" she asked, her breath forming a puffy cloud in the air.

"No, they just left. I forgot, they play canasta on Tuesday evenings." He stepped back to let her in, but she paused in the doorway. "Is that a problem?"

"Uh-uh, I just thought they'd be here."

Judging by her expression, that had been more of a hope than a thought.

"They'll be back later. Mom left stew for us, though. She thinks it's a great idea, by the way. The whole dating service. She's been angling for more grandkids. Hard to believe the Reign of Terror hasn't cured her of that."

"It hasn't cured you of wanting kids, has it?"

He cocked his head and took a second before answering, in case the question was more than just a casual curiosity. "No, I don't think so. It's definitely made me reevaluate how soon I want to have them, though."

She slipped in past him and beelined for the stairs. "Did you pack any dress clothes?"

"Not really, but my bedroom closet is still full of stuff that I never got around to clearing out when I moved."

"We'll see if any of that will work."

"How's your leg?" He trailed behind her up the steps, taking in the sway of her curvy hips under the heavy material. When she reached the top she hung a left, heading for his bedroom.

"Better, thanks. No bleeding, I changed the bandage this morning, and so far so good."

"Glad to hear it." She'd stopped in the center of the room and was aggressively ignoring the bed, her gaze taking in everything but. "Want me to take your coat?"

Their eyes met and held for a moment, and she wet her lips. "Sure." She slipped the coat from her shoulders and handed it him. He took in her appearance and held back a growl of appreciation. Black boots hugged her trim calves, and fitted gray jeans clung to her thighs, the outline of the bandage on her injured leg the only indication of yesterday's mishap. The short, red, off-the-shoulder sweater that capped off the look should have totally clashed with her hair. But it didn't. She looked bold and beautiful.

"You look great."

She glanced down at her clothes and smiled. "Thanks. The

sweater is part of my winter collection. I'd planned to do it in cashmere, but then fell in love with the way this mohair gave it such an interesting textural quality."

The pleasure she took in her work lit up her face, and he found himself wishing he knew more about clothes. Then maybe he could keep her talking. Unfortunately, he'd reached the bottom of the conversational well on fashion.

"Anyway, as you were saying, I do look pretty great. And that makes one of us." She wrinkled her nose, sweeping an assessing gaze over him from head to toe. "First we've got to lose the T-shirts. You've got a good body under there, and they definitely showcase that, but we can do better. Flaunt the goods but still let people know that you have some taste and more than eleven dollars in the bank to boot."

He glanced down at his shirt and frowned. "I don't get what the big deal is. It's just a T-shirt."

"Exactly," she said triumphantly, wagging a finger at him. "We can do better. Do you have any suits in here?" She turned to riffle through the tiny closet. Every so often, amid the scoffs and snorts, she handed him an item of clothing, most of which he hadn't worn in years. No surprise there. His parents had modernized some of the house since he'd left home, but his room was like one giant time capsule. The walls were still the same New York Giants blue that they'd been since his junior year of high school, and were riddled with pennants, posters, and foam fingers. Football and basketball trophies lined the shelves that ran the perimeter of the back the room. He was only glad he'd had the foresight to take down his framed Eagle Scout patch before she'd come over. No reason to give her more ammunition to support her theory about him.

She snapped her fingers a few feet in front of his face and called his name. "Hello? Anyone there?"

"I'm here. I was just thinking how ludicrous it was that you imagined I might get all decked out in a suit for coffee or a drink. It's not the eighteen hundreds. People go on dates in jeans all the time. I don't know what you think it is that I've been doing the last nine years, but I'm not a shut-in, Cat. I can dress myself."

She ignored him and held a brown sports coat up to his chest, sizing him up with a practiced eye. "This is perfect. Casual enough to seem like you don't care *that* much, for the girl who likes them aloof, but dressy enough to show you care, for the girl who likes a guy to put a little effort in." She pushed by him and tossed the jacket onto the bed. "You want to keep the T-shirt, I'll work with you. Wear it under this with those jeans." She gestured to the ones he had on. "You get dressed—I'm going to raid the bathroom for hair product and see what we can do."

She whirled away and he stared after her. "Hair product? You mean like gel or something? Do I really need that?"

She didn't bother to answer, the opening and closing of his bathroom cabinets answer enough.

Fine. None of this shit mattered anyway. The point was to keep her close, and he was definitely succeeding. He tugged off his T-shirt, then pulled a clean one out of his top drawer.

"I found some..." Cat stood in the doorway of the bathroom, can of mousse in her hand. Her gaze was glued to his naked chest and sent a sizzle straight to his cock.

"I thought you were wearing that T-shirt under the jacket."

Her voice sounded froggy and he bit back a grin. "I've been wearing it all day. I figured I'd get a clean one." He should've pulled the shirt over his head then, but if she was enjoying the show, who was he to stop her? He fisted the cotton, leaving his hand hanging by his side and her view unobstructed.

"What," she cleared her throat and tucked a strand of fiery hair behind one ear, "what does the tattoo represent?"

He was about to answer, then stalled. If he told her, it would derail her current fascination with his body, and he wasn't sure he was ready for her to stop looking at him like he was food.

He opened his mouth to tell her the same thing he'd told the last couple women he'd been with when they'd asked. Some lame bullshit about liking the pattern. But he found the words stuck in his craw. Instead he lifted his free hand to the symbol and held her electric-green eyes as he spoke. "Taken literally, it represents hope when things seem hopeless." He let his fingers drift to the next black character, tracing the still slightly raised flesh with his thumb.

He waited, wondering if she would press further...hoping she would. Hoping she wanted to know more about him, his life and what he'd been doing these past bunch of years.

She bit her lip, the indecision plain on her face. Then, she turned away.

Ouch.

"Cool. Finish getting dressed and we'll do your intro video. Then I have some ideas for still shots we can take. Do you have an ax?"

He nodded, yanking the T-shirt over his head. "Yeah."

Felt like one was lodged in his gut.

...

Cat set the video camera on the oak dining room table and peered at the screen. "Okay, sit up straight because you're slouching a little."

Shane straightened and frowned. "Is it even rolling yet?"

"No, but I want to make sure you fit in the frame when you're sitting right."

Shane didn't say anything, but that was nothing new. For the past twenty minutes, since their emotionally charged exchange in the bedroom, he'd been even quieter than normal. But in spite of her every effort not to, she couldn't stop thinking about his tattoo and the meaning behind it. Was it something to do with his job? Or about a woman?

That thought made the French cruller she'd eaten on the way over feel like a lump in her stomach. How stupid was that? Jealous over a woman who may or may not exist. Exactly the reason she never wanted to feel so much for a man. It did nothing but muddy the water. Good sex, companionship when needed, and common interests—those were the things she was looking for in a relationship. Get too caught up and someone ended up compromising until they'd compromised so much, they became someone else. A mirror for the person they were with.

A vision of her brilliant mother smiling her way through another student's painful performance of "Hot Cross Buns" flitted through her mind, and she shoved back the guilt that came with it.

Fuck. That.

"Can you see the script?" she asked Shane, shaking off the memories and melancholy to focus on the task at hand.

He leaned in to look at the iPad propped up near the camera and nodded. "Yup."

"Okay, readyyy, action!"

"Hello, ladies, how you doing?" He stopped abruptly and held up a hand. "Jesus, Cat, seriously? I'm not saying that. It makes me sound like a tool. What's next, my astrological sign?"

"No," she said, her tone sharp. "It was supposed to be funny. Like Joey from that old show *Friends*. Like, 'How *you* doin'?' If you think it's so bad, you come up with something better." She grabbed the iPad and covertly deleted the section about him being a Taurus and "strrrong like bull," which had seemed funny and kitschy when she'd written it, but less so now. "What do you want to open with, Casanova?"

"How about just, 'My name is Shane Decker.'"

"No salutation? Seems rude, but whatever." She adjusted the script and set the tablet back up so he could see it. "Okay, now just roll with it this time. If you don't like something, we can deal with it after. You're going to need a few retakes anyway, so let's use this first one as a trial to get you comfortable in front of the camera, tweak the lighting, etc. Pretend you're talking to really hot girl instead of a piece of equipment. Ready, aaand, action!"

Shane looked down at the table for so long, she was about to stop rolling and snap at him again, but then he lifted his head and pinned his stormy gaze on the camera. A wicked smile spread across his usually serious face. "Hi, my name is Shane Decker. I'm not much for chatter, so I'll get right to the point. I have some cue cards here telling me to describe my 'type,' but that's not me. I respect and love women. All types of women."

His voice rang with sincerity and Cat found herself leaning forward, literally on the edge of her seat.

"So if you think you're too tall and skinny but have a smile that makes people want to smile back? You're my type. Curvy and always trying to lose that last ten pounds, with a loud, bawdy laugh? You're my type. A little older than me, with some lifelines that look earned and the confidence that comes with age? My type. Life is short, and I want to spend it with someone who recognizes that, and takes happiness wherever they can find it. If you think I might be *your* type, send a message to Shane84, and we can meet for coffee."

The room was silent but for the dishwasher running in the background until Shane spoke again. "Was that okay?"

"Uh, yeah. You went off the grid a little, but it was fine." Fine? It was more than fine. What woman didn't want to hear that a sexy guy like Shane would love them even if they weren't perfect? The women at MeetMyMate.com were going to be salivating over him.

Which was great. Exactly what she'd been hoping for. Wasn't it? So why did she want to claw their collective, imaginary eyes out?

Shane smacked his hands on the table and stood. "Let's go get these pictures done and then we can eat."

She needed to stick to the plan. It was only a matter of time before all this excitement and anticipation she felt around him faded and things would be back to normal. It was nothing more than infatuation. The same she'd felt a million times before, except now—just like with that fat slice of strawberry cheesecake she'd almost managed to say no to the night before, after her kiss with Shane—it seemed larger than life because she was depriving herself of it. As soon as he was settled with someone new, and she got some space, she'd be thanking her lucky stars she dodged this bullet.

Note to self: buy another cheesecake on the way home.

She forced a cheery smile. "Sounds good. Where's your ax?"

"Probably in the shed. I forgot to ask, why do we need an ax again?" He led her toward the back door, tossing a glance over his shoulder.

"I don't know, I was thinking the ladies would like seeing you do something manly, like chop wood or something."

"Well, these aren't exactly my wood-chopping clothes," he said drily, glancing down. "Should I change?"

"Nah, just take the sports jacket off and go with the T-shirt and jeans."

They just stepped into the mudroom and he'd reached for his coat but paused. "It's like thirty degrees out."

"You're only going to be doing it for a few minutes," she reasoned. "Come on, I promise, I'll only take a couple shots, and we'll go right back inside. I won't put my coat on either."

He sighed and stripped off the jacket, slinging it over her shoulders. "No sense in us both freezing. But you've got five minutes to get the shot. I've been away too long, and my blood needs a little time to get used to this New England weather again."

She trailed out the back door behind him, swamped in his scent and oblivious to the cold as she tried to tear her gaze from his thick, broad shoulders. Instead she focused on the center of his back, but even that wasn't safe. The T-shirt clung tight enough that she could see the straight, deep indent of his spine flanked by the muscles that made a perfect V to his trim waist. She swallowed hard and blew out a steamy sigh.

Amended note to self: make it two cheesecakes.

• • •

Shane stood before the wide log on the chopping stump and looked up. "I say we've got about twenty minutes of daylight left, so let's get this done. Ready?"

Cat gave him the thumbs-up from her perch on the brick wall surrounding the patio. "Roger that."

She looked so frigging cute, red curls flapping in the icy breeze. He turned away, focusing his attention on the task at hand. He gripped the smooth, wooden handle and was just about to take a swing when he thought about the longing on her face when she'd seen him shirtless. Why the fuck not?

"Well, shit, if I'm going to do it, I'm going to do it right," he said, leaning the ax against his shin and yanking the T-shirt over his head. His whole body tightened in protest at the cold, but the look on her face as the camera hung from her limp hand, forgotten, was worth every ounce of pain.

He pretended not to notice and took the ax in hand again. Lining up, he set his feet, then took a swing. With a crack, the log splintered apart, falling into halves on the frosty grass.

"Did you get it?"

"Um, yeah." She nodded vigorously. "Yup. I got it."

"Are you sure? Because the camera's aimed at the ground."

She startled and peered down. "Well, it is now. It wasn't before. I just clicked it right before that. But, you know, sure. Let's do one more because this one's blurry."

Her nervous babble had him struggling not to grin. "Okay, ready?"

She nodded and pointed the lens in his direction. "Let 'er rip."

He lined up another piece of wood, then swung. It split cleanly and fell off the stump. "Can we go in now?"

She climbed down from the wall and walked over to him. "What do you think?"

She held the screen to his face and he glanced at the picture. It looked fine to him, but what did he know?

"Yes?"

She shook her head and rolled her eyes before starting toward the house. "Yes. You look great, which is so unfair. No tricks, no Photoshop, no makeup, stark natural light." He grabbed his shirt, catching up to her just in time to hear her grumble, "One shot, no one should look that good."

"So what next?"

"Next we get a couple more indoor stills, and put this and the video up on the site. I already wrote your bio, I've just got to cut and paste that into your profile. According to the guidelines, once everything is loaded, we wait for it to get reviewed and then it will go live. I'd say by the time we eat dinner and clean up, you'll be all set."

Forty-five minutes later, their bellies full of beef stew sopped up with thick slabs of buttered sourdough bread, they sat back in front of the computer with their coffee and Cat logged in.

"Okay, it looks like you're in." She clicked on his profile and the desktop *ding*ed. "And you have a message. Probably them welcoming you to the site, maybe some tips about how t—"

Before she could finish, it *ding*ed again. Then again.

"Maybe they have a welcoming committee," Cat said, clicking into the message center. Eleven new messages stared back at them, one of which was indeed a welcome from the president of MeetMyMate.com. The rest had numbers next to the subject lines, along with tiny thumbnail pictures.

All of them of women, lining up for a piece of him. Nuts.

Ding.

"Well," Cat said brightly, pushing away from the table to let him get in front of the screen. "Seems like there was a hole in the market for someone like you at this place. You're a hot commodity already."

"So what do I do now?"

"Click on their avatars, read their messages, and see if you like any of them."

"How will I know that from one message?"

Ding.

"You won't. But at least we can weed some out. The maybes we can put into a separate folder, and then the yeses you can set up short dates with."

Ding.

"Jesus H., can you turn that thing off?" she snapped. "It's very distracting."

He didn't care that she sounded like a shrew, because her reaction could only mean one thing. She was jealous. Satisfaction surged through him, and he vowed to redouble his efforts.

"Sure thing." He lowered the speakers, then clicked on the first message in the list. "Deedee Coruthers."

An image of a waifish blonde filled the screen. Cat looked

at it for a long moment, lips pursed. "Hmm…don't you think her right eye looks lazy? Like it's not really up on what the left one's doing, and doesn't care much to find out?" She made her eyes go slightly crossed. "It's off-putting in person, I bet, because you don't know which one to look at."

He looked at the photo more closely, and while Deedee wasn't a stunner, she didn't look cross-eyed. More like tired. "I guess a little…"

She didn't pay him any mind, already moving along to the next one. "Let's see, what about her? Sara Mitchell. She calls herself an artist. That probably means she doesn't have a job. She's also a vegan, which means you'd have to deal with her meat-shaming you."

He'd never been meat-shamed before. It sounded bad.

"And she probably does macramé," Cat continued. "So that crap will be hanging all over your house before you know it." She x-ed out Sara and pointed to another photo a few messages down. "She looks nice."

"Her?" he asked incredulously, sliding the cursor to blink under a masculine face.

"Yeppers. She's got an honest smile. I like that."

"Greta Doyle," he recited, clicking to enlarge her photo, which only succeeded in making her look even more like a man. "She likes sailing, waterskiing, and backpacking. Her favorite show is *Nancy Grace*, and she works as an occupational therapist."

"Sounds perfect for you."

"In what way?" he asked, openly frowning at her now.

"You like water sports."

His mind was inexorably drawn back to the time he and Cat had engaged in some water sports together, and for a second, he forgot what they were talking about.

"Shane?"

"Right. I do like water sports, but that's it? That's what

puts her in the keeper folder?"

"Sure. Common interests are huge in a relationship. Otherwise one person's always getting dragged around by the other and doing stuff they don't want to do, you know?"

He didn't know, but he nodded anyway. It seemed to him more that if two people liked being together, they made compromises sometimes and the rest of the time tried to find new things both people liked to do, but there was no point in arguing. He had no interest in dating any of these women, opposite or not, so what did it matter who he corresponded with? As long as he let them know up front he was looking for friendship only, there wouldn't be a problem. But he had to make sure some of them were attractive enough to make Cat jealous. "Okay. Maybe she's just not photogenic. Who else you got for me?"

She sipped her coffee and clicked on to the next one. "Courtney Lockhart DeLollis. Hmm…"

Courtney was quite the looker. Long, honey-blond hair, wide-set hazel eyes.

"Nope." Cat shook her head, and moved to close the photo. He covered her hand with his to stop her.

"What's wrong with this one?"

"Vapid. You can see it in the eyes. Dull. Not quite focused. If I were to guess what she was thinking right now, it would be 'I like turtles' or 'I wonder what Kim Kardashian is doing right now' or something."

She looked dead serious, but that couldn't be right. "You can tell that from looking at her eyes in one picture? How is that even possible?"

"It's just a feeling. She looks like a nitwit. It's your choice, though. If you want to spend an evening discussing the merits of turtles, go for it."

He stared at her hard, but she steadfastly ignored him. "Cat."

"What?" She kept her gaze locked on the monitor, but her fingers tapped a nervous beat on the desk.

"Is this what you do?" he asked.

"What do you mean?"

"Don't play dumb. Is this what you do to guys you date? Look for flaws?"

"Oh, honestly, now you sound like Lacey. That's not what I'm doing. I'm just trying to save you some time." She looked down at her watch. "Speaking of which, I've got to go."

Running again. A tense moment passed while he debated whether to let her off so easily, but eventually he stood. They'd kissed last night; she'd gotten jealous today. They were making slow, steady progress. He had all the time in the world. "Okay. I'll get your coat. You want to help me weed through some of these tomorrow?"

She stood and stretched, the move baring enough of her sleek tummy to distract him from hearing the front end of her response. "...to go bungee jumping tomorrow, but I think I'm just going to cancel. I have a couple things to do in the morning, but you can come by my place around noon if you want."

"Why cancel the jump? You've been dying to do it, so do it."

"I was supposed to go with a girl from work, but something came up and she can't make it. The thing is, it's a two-person rig, so if I went alone I'd be paired with a stranger. Just won't be as much fun."

"I'll go with you."

She stared at him dubiously. "It doesn't really seem like your thing."

"I spend a lot of time in risky conditions for work, so it's not something I'd necessarily go out of my way to do for pleasure, but I'd do it to support a friend if she didn't want to go alone." She hadn't said no yet, but she was about to. "I can tell you're looking for a reason to say no, but I'm not sure why. Friends help each other. Unless you're afraid?"

"Afraid? Not a chance. I've gone skydiving, parasailing, hang gliding, swimming with sharks." She ticked each one off on her fingers. "I'm not scared to bungee-jump."

"I didn't say you were. I was thinking maybe you were afraid of bungee jumping...with me." He stepped closer. Close enough to see her pupils dilate and the pulse pound in her throat.

"What's that supposed to mean?" The column of her neck worked as she swallowed, and any thoughts of letting her off easy crashed and burned. He closed the remaining distance between them, pressing forward until her back was against the wall.

"You tell me."

Chapter Seven

What was the question again?

Hell if she could remember. His mouth was so close, his big body crowding her, frazzling her already-frayed nerves.

"I don't want you to kiss me," she heard herself murmur, even as she stretched onto her tiptoes to get closer to his lips.

"That isn't what I asked you," he said, tracing the line of her cheekbone with his finger. "I asked why you're afraid of me."

"I'm not afraid of you."

"You are. And I want to know why." His lips followed the path his finger created, brushing along her skin like a whisper.

"I—I just don't want to get involved with someone who—" She gasped when his warm breath caressed her earlobe.

"Someone who?"

She shouldn't answer. It would only make things worse if he knew, but the words were out before she could stop them. "Someone who makes me feel like this."

The groan seemed torn from his throat, and he bent low, wrapping his strong arms around her. The instant his mouth touched hers, the dam broke. Everything she'd been feeling rushed forward like a tidal wave. She twined her arms around his neck and plastered herself against him, reveling in the feel of his tightly bunched muscles. His tongue stroked hers in a primal rhythm that made her stomach clench with need. His mouth was magic, and the memory of him between her thighs was almost too much to bear.

She slid a restless hand into his hair and tugged, desperate for more. His palms drifted lower, cupping her ass and lifting her clear off the ground. Instinctively, she wrapped her legs around his hips, crying out against his mouth when the hard, thick length of him pressed against the spot already so primed for his touch. It was sublime, and she fluttered her hips against his in a wordless plea for more. He sucked gently on her bottom lip, then rolled his pelvis, wringing a moan from her when his erection rocked against her clit harder this time. He drew back and repeated the motion, again and again, fanning the flames higher and hotter, almost out of control.

He pulled his mouth from hers to press soft kisses along her jaw, down her neck. "God, you are so fucking sexy," he murmured, gripping her ass tighter, using his hold to grind her against his rock-hard cock in a way that had the blood pounding in her ears. She was one firm touch, one clever finger away from a mind-blowing orgasm.

"Hold on tight," he growled.

She did, gripping his thick shoulders with all her might and locking her legs tighter around his waist.

"Good girl." He pulled away from the wall, and she whimpered at the loss of pressure between her legs. She quieted a second later when he sat her on the dining room table, urging her to lean back on her hands. "I just need to see you this time." His voice was all grit and need, and she quivered, powerless to deny him. He traced the skin on her stomach reverently, then slowly lifted her sweater higher.

"Beautiful," he muttered, tracing the scalloped edge of her strapless black bra. With a flick of his fingers he released the closure, and it fell to the side.

The chilly air hit her, and her nipples tightened even more, but it was the heat in his eyes that had her whole body quivering.

"Jesus. That's fucking—" He broke off and dropped to her, his hot mouth closing over one nipple and sucking.

"Shane!" She moaned, tossing her head back, letting the heat and pressure of his lips and tongue drag her closer to the edge.

He pulled away and blew on the distended tip. "Peach. I wondered if the memory was skewed or it was a trick of the moonlight. I love peach. And so sensitive." He nipped her, murmuring his approval when she gasped. "Let your legs down."

She obeyed, releasing the death grip she had around him to let her legs dangle over the edge of the table. He stepped back a few inches and cupped her denim-covered pelvis, rubbing her in slow, firm circles. She bit her lip to keep from chanting his name when he lowered his mouth back toward her nipple.

"Can you come like this?" His warm breath washed over her, and she wanted to drag him closer until his lips were on her again. "I think you can. Come for me, Cat," he murmured, and closed his mouth over the straining bud, sucking and licking, matching the relentless rhythm of the sensual massage between her thighs.

"Oh my God," she groaned, every nerve ending at attention, the sensation hurtling her toward release. He pinched her nipples sharply between his teeth, and the pleasure-pain sent her flying. The waves of ecstasy rolled over, and she bit her lip to keep from sobbing. Through the buzzing in her ears, she heard Shane's hums of encouragement. She also heard the sound of a car door slamming shut.

She froze but for the fading spasms of her orgasm, and her eyes popped open. Then, a second car door slammed. This one hit her like a slap, clearing away the haze of lust.

"Your parents," she whispered furiously, pushing him away and yanking her sweater down.

He lifted his head, and stared at her blankly, eyes hot with need. "What?"

"Your parents are home!" She shoved him hard and slid off the table, trying to ignore the little flip her stomach was doing at the sight of his firm lips swollen from the kissing and sucking.

"Fix...that," she said, pointing urgently at the massive erection that was attempting to burst through his zipper. She grabbed her bra and stuffed it into her pocket.

"Okay, let's just have a seat in the living room and stay calm." He straightened the centerpiece they'd manage to displace and led her the few feet to the drop-in living room. They'd just sat down in front of the fireplace when the door opened.

Cat ran a quick hand through her mussed hair and worked up a smile.

"Hey guys," Shane called to his parents as they stepped into the hallway. He adjusted his jeans with final tug before they rounded the corner. "Did you win or what?"

"We split," Martha Decker said, stepping into the room with a smile. "Hey there, sweetheart," she said when she caught sight of Cat. She ambled over and pulled her up for a baby-powder-scented hug. "How are your parents doing?"

"They're good, thanks for asking." She resisted the urge to fidget under the older woman's sharp gaze. Were her lips puffy, too? She quelled the need to touch them, knowing it would only draw attention to them if they were.

Shane's dad came into the room carrying an empty Crock-

Pot. "Hello, Mary Catherine. Good to see you again." He set the pot on the dining room table and shifted his gaze between Shane and her. "So what are you kids up to? You find my boy a wife yet?"

"Oh, Aaron, stop teasing them. He's not going to find a wife on the computer, are you, Shane? He's just looking to make some nice new friends." She slung her purse on the arm of a wing chair and reached down to pat her son's cheek. "You feel a little warm," she said with a frown. "Are you getting sick?"

Cat kept her eyes on Shane, hoping no one was looking at her because her face was on fire.

Shane shook his head. "No, although I count that as a miracle what with the climate change. Your hands are just cold from being outside."

She released him and pulled off her down-filled white coat. "Did you both have stew?" she asked, her eyes flicking to Cat.

"Yes, thank you. It was delicious."

"I made apple pie for dessert, if you'd like some."

She wasn't one to say no to pie, but the need to get out of there trumped her sweet tooth. "I appreciate the offer, but I'm stuffed. Can I take a rain check?"

"I'll do you one better," Martha said. "You can take a slice home. Follow me." She pulled Cat to her feet and led her by the hand into the newly renovated gourmet kitchen. "Have a seat while I cut you a piece and wrap it."

"Thanks, I'm sure I'll be thrilled to have it around midnight when the fridge starts calling me." She sat at the table and watched Martha bustle around.

"So tell me, dear," she said, opening a drawer and pulling out a pie server. "What's going on between you and my son?"

Cat stared at the older woman in shock, hoping she'd misheard.

"You both looked pretty out of sorts and mussed when we walked in, but then I thought, that can't be right. You're trying to fix him up with other women, aren't you? So what gives?"

Cat started to answer but stopped when she couldn't form a coherent response. The ambush had been laid masterfully, and even now, her captor held her in place with nothing more than a cheerful smile.

She tried again. "I—I'm not sure what to say, Mrs. Decker. I like Shane a lot, but…" She shrugged helplessly, wondering if she looked even half as uncomfortable as she felt. "It's really complicated."

"I have a good understanding about matters of the heart, you know," Martha continued, transferring a wedge of pie onto a sheet of aluminum foil. "Sometimes people think couples who have only ever been with each other don't know how complicated love and romance can be, but that's the furthest thing from the truth. Aaron and I have spent the past forty years making it work through some pretty trying times, and I know one thing for sure. Nothing is so complicated that it can't be worked out if you really love each other."

She folded the foil into a neat triangle around the pie, then slipped it into a paper lunch bag. "I've always thought there was something interesting brewing between the two of you. Call it mother's intuition. I know I'm overstepping, but I've got to ask…" Martha's blue gaze pinned her to the spot. "Do you love my son, Mary Catherine?"

Cat's brain whirred like a top, and she tried to think of what she could possibly say to escape this situation without making it worse. Her feet were already on the ground, her body in flight mode, when Shane walked in, saving her from coming up with a reply.

"I grabbed your coat." He held it out expectantly. "Ready to go?"

She popped out of the chair like a jack-in-the-box, relief making her knees weak, and took the bag Martha held out for her.

"Thanks so much for the pie, Mrs. Decker."

"It was nice see you again, dear." Martha's wink held just a hint of a challenge. "Don't be a stranger."

"Will do! I mean, will do not be a stranger, because I'm not. We already know each other…and stuff." She pulled her coat on and followed Shane to the front door. "Good night, Mr. Decker," she said as they passed him where he sat at the table laying out a crossword puzzle.

"'Night," he said without looking up.

Cat's hot face fairly sizzled when they stepped into the frosty night. She walked ahead of Shane to the driveway where her car was parked, hoping he would take pity on her and just let her go. When he opened her door and she slid into the driver's seat, she neatly managed to avoid all contact with his body, but he stood by the open door while she turned the key in the ignition.

"My mom pulled the old separate-one-from-the-herd trick. Sorry about that," he said, although the half smile suggested he wasn't all that sorry. "By the time I saw it coming, it was too late to stop her."

She pursed her lips and tucked a strand of hair behind her ear. "It's not your fault. And you did good getting the coat from upstairs and running interference at the end there. She had me in a real spot for a minute."

"I heard right before I walked in."

Oh jeez. She leaned over and started fiddling with the radio. "Yeah, well, it was no big deal. Just a mom watching out for her son. Speaking of which, you'd better go inside before she gets the wrong idea about us."

"And what would the right idea be?" he asked, his tone mocking, as if he knew what her answer would be, and he was daring her to come up with something more original.

Too bad for him that she was done with dares. "That we're just friends and that's all we're ever going to be."

"Right."

"Shane, I'm sorry for...everything. Inside. It shouldn't have happened." Her body was still warm and loose from her release, and the words left a sour taste in her mouth. "Correction. I shouldn't have allowed it to happen. I don't know what's the matter with me lately. What I do know is that, when I'm thinking straight, I don't want this." She gestured back and forth between them. "It's not what I'm looking for." She waited for him to argue and scrambled to get her defenses ready, but the argument never came.

"Okay," he said with a short nod.

The fact that he accepted her response without question made her feel like crying, and the fact that it made her feel like crying made her want to punch something. She had to get out of there fast, before she did something even stupider than she already had.

"So I guess I'll see you later," she said, clicking on her seat belt and eyeing his arm on the door pointedly.

"Sounds good. Are we going bungee jumping tomorrow or did you want me to come by to go over some more responses?"

"I don't think I'm going to do the jump. It's going to be really cold out anyway, and my knee is still sore, so I'll do it another time." The cold-weather excuse was bullshit. Actually, so was the issue of being paired with a stranger. She didn't care a lick about that. She was just so preoccupied with thoughts of Shane and all the stupid girls e-mailing him, she knew she wouldn't be able to enjoy herself if she went. They weren't even an item, and the soul-sucking—although unintentional—was already starting. Imagine if they were together for real? She turned the key in the ignition. "And I'll let you know about stopping by."

"Sure thing." He nodded and gave her car door a pat, slammed it shut, then turned and jogged lightly up the walkway without a backward glance.

He seemed fine, which was good. She didn't want to hurt him with her erratic behavior. She only wished she was handling it all as well as he was. But what the hell with this new Shane? All of a sudden the guy who'd followed her around for a year scaring off potential boyfriends, arguing with her over how many drinks was too many or why skinny-dipping at night was a bad idea, wanted to go bungee jumping with her? Talk about confusing. She felt like her head was going to explode, because nothing was the same as she remembered it.

Except the sexual chemistry. That was good then, and it was good now. Which made it even worse. Less than a week since they'd slept together, and so far, Operation Forget About Shane was going about as well as the maiden voyage of the Titanic. She could see the iceberg ahead but just couldn't seem to steer clear of it. Maybe it was time to abandon ship. Just stop trying to fix him up and avoid him altogether. But the thought left her feeling just as miserable as the alternative.

She leaned her forehead on the cold, leather steering wheel and blinked back tears. "Shit."

...

Shane crept back into the house, hoping to sneak past his mom, get his keys, and get the hell out of Dodge before she cornered him. It was a pipe dream, though, and the second he picked up his keys from the glass bowl in the foyer, she appeared like a meddlesome specter in the night.

"Heading out?"

"I was going to, yeah," he said, still hanging on to the slim hope that she'd let him off easy.

She sat down on the long, floral couch and beckoned him over. "Sit with me for five minutes and tell me what's going on with you and Mary Catherine and why it looks like it's bothering you so much."

Fuck if he knew. The sight of Cat sprawled on the dining room table ran through his mind, and he nearly groaned. This getting all worked up and going nowhere shit was for the birds, but he certainly wasn't going to confess that to his mother. Telling her that he was crazy about Cat would cause even more problems, because then she would be relentless. He shot for vague. "I can't answer that right now. I don't know myself."

"It's something, then. That's good. I was a little worried my instincts were getting rusty."

"Nope, no rust there." She wasn't going to quit, so he bit the bullet and went to sit next to her.

"What do you intend to do about her?"

"Right now? Nothing. Wait for her to figure out what she wants."

"If you wait on her and she's confused, you could be waiting forever. And if you let her have you when she wants you but let her throw up a wall the rest of the time, then there's no incentive for her to make up her mind." She leaned forward and patted his hand gently. "My suggestion? Go on your dates using this computer service, and see what happens. Maybe that will make Mary Catherine realize she could lose out on a chance with a great guy and she'll gain some clarity. Or maybe it won't, but you'll meet someone you like and that will be okay, too."

He didn't know about that last part, since the idea of coming out the other end of this with someone other than Cat had no appeal for him at all, but the rest fell nicely into line with his own thinking. Maybe he'd stay in tonight after all.

"Thanks for the talk, Ma."

She smiled and got to her feet. "Your father and I are going to watch our show on the BBC in the den. Come join us if you like. And think about what I said. Don't let this girl lead you around by the nose. There's no point in her buying the bronco if the rides are free."

She shuffled off, leaving him alone with that pearl of wisdom, wishing he could scrub it from his brain. But damn if she didn't have a point.

With a sigh, he tossed his keys on the coffee table, then went upstairs to his room, grabbing his laptop from the armchair in the corner when he passed. Sitting at the pine desk he'd had since high school, he opened his computer and logged on. After a cursory glance of his work e-mails—seemed he'd missed the cave-in of a tunnel during a Calabasas mudslide, no casualties, thank God—he entered the MeetMyMate.com site and was instantly bombarded with messages. Too bad the one that played on a loop in his head was the one he wished he could delete most.

We're just friends, and that's all we're ever going to be.

"Fine, Cat. You win," he muttered under his breath. He scrolled through the e-mails until he found the one he was looking for and then clicked on the instant message box.

The light was green, indicating the sender was online, so he whipped off a quick introduction. The cursor blinked for a long while before a response box popped up.

Hey, it's nice to "meet" you, too. I'm so glad you decided to get in touch!

Chapter Eight

Cat stared listlessly at the TV and took another halfhearted bite of cold toast. It had been two days since she'd talked to Shane, and it had been the most miserable two days of her life. He'd left a message yesterday, but she hadn't answered. She needed to not be around him for a while. He wreaked havoc on her emotions, and she couldn't think when he was close by. Unfortunately, now things had gotten so bad that she couldn't stop thinking about him, even when he wasn't around.

Maybe it was nothing. Maybe it would be like the time Lacey had gotten the gorgeous pink bike for Christmas when they were eight. It had a bell and a basket and little purple flowers painted on it. Cat had coveted that damned bike so much, there were points she wondered if it would just splinter into a thousand pieces from the force of her want. Until the day Lacey let her ride it. She tore up and down the street, feeling like a big shot. But after twenty minutes of hard riding, she realized the bell jangled every time she hit a bump, and the brakes weren't nearly as responsive as hers. Overall, it was a total letdown. Maybe if she rode Shane hard for twenty more minutes, she'd realize that what she felt for him was nothing more than another case of pink bike syndrome.

As much as she was confused about her feelings, though, the one point she was crystal clear on was that there was no way in hell she was going to be able to help him pick a girlfriend. Picturing him with another woman suddenly seemed about as appetizing as eating maggoty cheese. Wondering if he was touching them the way he'd touched her. Kissing them with that wicked, sexy mouth.

"Argh," she groaned, and covered her eyes with her hands, trying to scrub away the thoughts. Eventually, she'd have to tell him she wasn't going to help him anymore, but for now, the word of the day was procrastinate.

Her cell phone vibrated on the glitter-encrusted coffee table. She reached for it, heart stuttering until she saw Lacey's name flash across the screen. *Not Shane.*

She cleared her throat and pressed the green call button. "Hey."

"Hey. What are you doing?"

"Just hanging around, you?" Cat had managed to avoid seeing her for the last few days in hopes of letting the Shane situation run its course, but Lacey hadn't gotten a chance to grill her the way she'd wanted. There was no way she was going to be able to hold her off much longer.

"I have a couple classes today, but I'm free later. Want to go out to dinner tonight?"

Cat stared down at her toast, the smear of jam coagulating with an oil slick of melted margarine gone cold, and she shrugged. Maybe she could drown her sorrows in some good food and beer. It was her vacation, after all, and so far she'd done none of the fun things she'd planned. Getting out couldn't make her feel worse than staying in.

"Sure.

"Okay, I'll swing by and get you around seven. I can't stay

out too late, though. Galen and I are leaving for New York City early tomorrow morning. We're going skating and then I'm taking him to see *Mamma Mia*."

Cat groaned. "Aren't you sick of that yet?"

"Nope."

"Well give the poor bastard my condolences." She felt bad for her brother having to sit through that, but better him than her. Every man for himself. In fact, maybe this phone call was a sign of some sort. A reminder that even happy couples had to do a shitload of compromising.

"You're just jealous because I didn't invite you," Lacey said. "Oh! And I heard Shane has a date from that site already, huh?"

The nugget of self-righteousness faded as a wave of despair hit her, leaving her chilled from the inside out. She pulled her sweater tighter around her. "Where'd you hear that?" Too soon. It was too fucking soon.

"Galen."

"Did he say with who?"

"He did, but I can't remember her name."

She strived for a casual tone. "Maybe Deedee? Or Greta?" She squeezed her eyes closed and mentally crossed her fingers. She'd even be okay with the macramé chick, as long as it wasn't—

"I want to say Cari…no, Courtney? Was that one of the choices?"

Shit. A vision of the beautiful blonde who, in truth, looked anything but vapid, floated before her eyes, and Cat's stomach roiled. "Okay, yeah. I think that was one of them. Well, good for him. I'm sure they'll have a great time together."

"They were going to Sully's for wings or something." There was a long pause and Lacey sighed. "Why are you doing this, Cat?"

"I'm not doing anything."

In spite of her words, she didn't have the strength to mask the misery in her voice, and Lacey's derisive snort echoed over the line. "I don't understand why it would be such a terrible thing to admit you dig Shane and give it a go."

You wouldn't understand, she wanted to reply, but bit her tongue. Lacey had been under her mother's thumb for so long that falling in love with Galen had been more freeing than anything she'd ever known. Cat had been free her whole life. Getting into a relationship with a guy like Shane, who already was taking up way too much real estate in her brain and her heart, would smother her until she had nothing left but her man and a sad violin case on a shelf.

"I don't know how much clearer I can be, Lace. It's not going to happen. Now do you want to go out to eat or what?"

Silence crackled over the line before Lacey broke it by chirping, "Sure. Let's go to Sully's, too. You love it there."

And run into Shane? "No way. I'm not doing that." Even as the words left her mouth, she wanted to take them back, but Lacey was already pouncing like a cat on a rat.

"If you're not interested in Shane, then why would it be a big deal? I'm confused, Cat. Either you like him and don't want to see him with another woman, or he doesn't matter. Which is it?"

Little Lacey Drawers thought she could play with the big girls now and muscle her into admitting something she had firmly filed in the "deny at all costs" file, huh? She was out of her league. "You want to go to Sully's? Fine by me. I want to see what he's wearing anyway. I told him to stop with the T-shirts all the time. He's not in college anymore, right?"

Lacey's tone grew hesitant. "We're really going to go there?"

Rule number one, Lacey Drawers. Don't wave the gun around if you don't want to use it. "Absolutely. See you at seven."

After they said their good-byes, she set her cell phone on the coffee table and hunkered deeper into the couch cushions. Part of her dreaded seeing Shane with his date. Especially if she was as pretty as her picture. But an even bigger part of her was oddly relieved. Sitting at home not knowing what was going on—if he was laughing at Courtney's jokes or if she had a fat ass—would have been way worse. Her imagination would have run wild, and by the end of the night she would have convinced herself the woman spent her days curing cancer and shitting gumdrops.

No. Getting to see what was happening was definitely better.

So why did it feel so frigging bad?

...

Shane popped a chip smothered in spinach dip into his mouth and chewed while he scanned the room. The kitschy neighborhood bar was pretty dead this early on a Thursday night, and the relative quiet made conversation easy. He locked eyes with Courtney and gave her his full attention. "So you're a nurse. Tell me about that. You enjoy it?"

Her pretty face lit up, and she leaned in across the table. "So much. I work in the ER now, and I love the fast pace. It's also good for someone like me because it's easier to stay detached. The patients are only with us for immediate issues before they're either released or transferred. Before you can get too involved, they roll out or go home, and another stretcher rolls in, and the latest and greatest crisis takes center stage."

He knew all about crisis, and he knew a fair bit about trying not to get involved and how hard it was not to. "Where did you work before the ER?"

She dimmed visibly and sat back. The change was so

abrupt, he wished he could retract the question.

"Pediatrics."

One-word answer; it was plain on her face that there was more to that story. Something—maybe everything—had hit her hard there. He could only imagine the things she'd seen. Things that still haunted her. He knew the feeling and took her nonverbal cue to mind his own business.

"It's nice to meet someone who likes their job," he said, swiping his napkin over a drop of dip on the lacquered table. "So many people dread Mondays. Me, I've been on vacation a week and, although I needed the break, I'm kind of itching to get back out there."

Courtney took a sip of her merlot, then nodded. "I totally agree. Life's too short to waste doing something you hate."

She was right there. Life was too fucking short. Too short to work at a job you hated, too short to miss out on opportunities or have regrets. He liked this woman. They'd been hanging out for a couple hours now, and the conversation had moved along at a steady, comfortable clip. No weird revelations, no awkward pauses. They both had high-pressure jobs and enjoyed physical activity as an outlet for stress. She was pretty, smart, caring…hell, on paper, they were a perfect match.

His thoughts turned to Cat as they had a dozen times over the past hour. Too bad her formula wasn't as foolproof as she thought. He and Courtney may have all the boxes ticked off in the compatibility department, but he felt no chemistry with her at all. Zilch. And if he was any kind of judge, he'd say she felt the same way. Maybe he'd set the stage for that during their IM chat when he'd explained that he wasn't in the market for a girlfriend. That he was re-acclimating himself to the area and was just looking for someone to hang out with, go to dinner, catch a movie or a concert sometime. She was happy to hear it since she'd gotten out of a difficult relationship and was looking for companionship more than love herself. He was satisfied with his choice, felt he'd made a friend, and it sure as hell beat sitting at home wondering whether Cat was going to get some balls and call him. Not to mention, when she found out which woman he'd picked to go out with, she was *not* going to like it.

The door swung open, sending an icy draft over their table, and Courtney shivered.

"Ooh, nice boots," she whispered, gaze glued to the doorway.

Shane didn't have to wait long to see the objects of her admiration because two women walked by a few seconds later, one sporting fitted tan boots with a wicked-looking heel.

"Those?"

"Yeah. Want," she whimpered in a funny little voice.

He laughed and took another look at the boots that were eating up space between them and the bar. They were pretty nice. If he was being honest, the whole package was pretty nice. Curvy, denim-encased legs led to a nicely rounded bottom that was framed by a tan, fitted leather jacket.

He took a harder look at the ass.

Jesus. It was Cat.

The two women reached the bar fifteen yards away and selected their seats, which happened to face his table.

"Holy shit."

"What's the matter?" Courtney asked, concern furrowing her brow.

"Nothing, ah…"

Lacey waved enthusiastically from her stool, and Cat gave a crooked grin and a finger wiggle. Maybe he was reading too much into it, but her smile seemed stiff and a little sad.

He waved back, brain on overdrive trying to make sense of this development. It couldn't be a coincidence, could it? They all loved Sully's, so it wasn't impossible. Still, neither Lacey nor Cat had looked surprised to see him, and they hadn't stopped at the table to say hi, which was weird. And he *had* told Galen what was going on with Cat and where he would be tonight with the hope it would filter to her eventually, but he hadn't expected this. What did she think she'd accomplish by showing up?

Either way, here she was, and he wasn't complaining. It had to mean something.

"Who's that?" Courtney asked.

"Oddly enough, that's the woman I was telling you about earlier."

To her credit, Courtney didn't whip her head back around to get another look. Instead, she went for a stealthy, reach-for-the-purse maneuver that allowed her to look over her shoulder without it seeming obvious. If Cat's whole vapid-turtle theory hadn't been blown out of the water in the first half hour of conversation, it sure was now. This chick was quick.

Cat had taken off her jacket, and he lost track of his thoughts for a moment. She wore a cropped sweater in dark blue that skimmed over her breasts like a lover before ending abruptly right above her navel.

"The redhead, right?"

He dragged his attention back to Courtney and nodded. "Yeah."

"This is the woman who doesn't want to be with you?" she asked, her tone incredulous.

"That's what she tells me."

"Well, her coming here dressed like that when you're here with me tells me something different. Either she's in serious denial about her feelings for you, or you have a crazy woman on your hands and might want to consider carrying a weapon."

Shane laughed and felt the heat of Cat's stare drilling

into him. "We've known each other for years, and I'm fairly confident it's not the latter."

Courtney's hazel eyes searched his face. "And you're really hoping it's the former."

He nodded. "She's special."

"I wondered why you said in your message that you were just looking to make new friends. At first I thought it was a line. Guy code for, 'Not looking for love, just looking to get laid.'" She laughed and it was pleasant, but nothing like Cat's full-belly laugh, which he hadn't heard enough of lately.

"So why did you want to come out with me then?" It was the logical question, although he was only half-listening to the answer as he tried not to watch Cat trying not to watch him.

She shrugged. "You had a nice face, and I figured if I sensed a player vibe I could always have one drink and leave. Once I got here, I realized you were sincere. I've lived here for almost two years, but was with someone that whole time, and he wasn't big on socializing." Her tone was light, but she'd begun to fidget with the rim of her wineglass, and it was obvious they were treading on uncomfortable territory. "I thought it was time to settle in, make friends, create roots. I'd never been able to do that before when I was with my ex."

She trailed off, and he wondered if he should ask about her why that was. Luckily, their waitress came over and asked if they were ready to order their meals, breaking the tension. When she walked away, his cell phone buzzed. He tugged it from his jacket pocket and read the message.

Don't worry, stud. I only came to see what ur wearing n make sure ur not boring her to death. Just pretend I'm not here.

Right. Like that was going to happen. But he found a smile tugging at his lips because, for whatever reason, she was here and she was obviously jealous and trying to play it off like she wasn't.

I think we're in the clear. Mostly talking turtles, which, incidentally, we both find fascinating.

"Sorry about that," he said to Courtney as he slipped the phone back into his pocket. "Did you want to play darts while we wait for our food?"

Cat's uninhibited laugh sounded from the bar, and he couldn't hold back the grin. She must have liked his turtle joke.

"I take it that was your girl texting," Courtney asked, nothing but genuine curiosity on her face.

He gave her a sheepish smile. "It was, sorry about that. Didn't mean to be rude, but I don't think it will happen again."

"Unless, of course, we make it happen again…" She waggled an eyebrow suggestively, the move so at odds with her round, angelic face that he laughed.

"I know the look of a woman with a plan. I'm just not smart enough to figure out what that plan is."

Her smile was pure evil. "You want to know how to get a woman to admit she has feelings for you? Get a *different* woman to admit she does first." She pushed back her chair and tossed her napkin onto the table.

Chapter Nine

Did her laugh have to be so fucking musical? Cat whirled her shot glass in a circle, watching the liquid form an amber cyclone. When it slowed its rotation, she shot the contents back in one swallow.

"They seem to be having a good time," Lacey said, spearing a cherry tomato with her fork.

"Yeah. Great for him."

Lacey leaned forward to take the empty glass from Cat's unresisting fingers. "If you really feel that way, then why are you drinking like it's your job?"

"I'm not. I always drink like this on a"—she peered down at her watch through bleary eyes—"Thursday evening."

"Sure you do."

"I guess I just can't figure why, with at least two dozen perfectly good empty chairs in the place, she needs to share his." Stupid Courtney's stupid laugh rang through the stupid room again, and Cat wanted to stab something. "Or what is so-o-o fuckin-n-n-g funny."

The pair had been laughing it up for the past hour, and

Cat couldn't wait for Lacey to finish her damned salad so she could get out of there. The sight of Courtney forking a bite of pie into Shane's mouth had almost sent her over the edge. Not to mention the woman was wearing the exact Michael Kors blouse she'd been eyeing at Barneys the week before but hadn't been able to afford. It was like salt in an already excessively salty wound.

"Oop, you got your wish," Lacey mumbled around a mouthful of lettuce and cheese. "She's off his lap now. They're getting up."

The small acoustic band that had been playing folk music in the corner had just switched it up to something slow and jazzy and from her peripheral, Cat could see several couples make their way to the small, makeshift dance floor.

"Are they going to dance?" she whispered urgently, keeping her eyes locked on the bowl of honey-roasted peanuts in front of her.

Lacey opened her mouth to answer but Cat turned and smashed her hand over Lacey's lips before she could. "Wait. Don't tell me. Just wink."

Lacey pulled away from her grasp and rolled her eyes. "Can't I nod or shake my head instead? You know I'm not a good winker."

"I don't care what you do. Just don't say it out loud. I don't want to hear it."

She knew it was silly, and totally irrational, but that had been par for the course from the second she'd gotten into his bed. She was losing her mind. If this was what opening herself up to a person and letting them in felt like, she'd been right to avoid it. So far, it sucked.

"Well, I'm not sure what to do in this situation," Lacey murmured. "They're not dancing but…"

"But what? Are they leaving? Are they holding hands? Does he have his arm arou—"

"Hey, Shane!" Lacey said, louder than necessary. She slid off the barstool to stand with Shane and his date, who, Cat realized as she spun her chair around, were directly behind them. "And you must be Courtney. So nice to meet you. I hope we didn't make things awkward for you guys." Lacey's smile was so sweet it could have charmed the pants off Willy Wonka.

Courtney smiled back, her perfect white teeth gleaming like freshwater pearls under the fluorescent pendant lights. "Not at all. It's good to see that he has friends who care about him so much that they want to check out his dates. Only a good man would inspire such loyalty."

So not vapid. In fact, her hazel eyes sparkled with intelligence. It figured.

Cat remembered her manners and held out a hand. "Cat, nice to meet you."

"You, too," Courtney said, taking the proffered hand and shaking it lightly before releasing it.

"Where's Galen tonight?" Shane asked, seemingly unconcerned when Courtney slung a casual arm around his trim waist.

"He's out with Rafe. They worked all day installing a new hot tub at his place, so Rafe took him out to eat. They'll probably end up here eventually."

"We're actually on our way out," Courtney said. "Going to hit a friend's art showing at the gallery on Ninth and then..." She shrugged a bare shoulder.

And then? What the hell was that supposed to mean? She could feel the fake smile frozen on her face, which was good, because she was a hairbreadth from a snarl. She picked up her beer and took a long swallow.

You wanted this. This is all on you, she reminded herself.

"Yeah, well, you two have fun," she said, and resolutely turned her attention back to the peanuts.

"You guys, too. See you Monday for game night?"

Cat felt the heat of his gaze, but still didn't look up.

"If not sooner," Lacey said and stood to hug Shane. "Drive safe."

A minute later, they were gone, and Cat broke eye contact with the nuts. Oddly, even they seemed to be judging her from their lofty little bowl. "Well, that was fun," she muttered under her breath.

"Was it? Because it didn't look fun from where I was sitting," Lacey said with a grim twist of her lips. "I don't understand you, Cat. You guys are obviously crazy about each other. Would it be so bad to admit that and give it a try?"

Cat shook her head and slumped forward to rest her chin in her hands. "I don't even know anymore. I feel like I can't win. I'm miserable now, but I'd be even more miserable if I did give in. There's no halfway with a guy like Shane."

"Some guys are worth the whole shebang, Cat."

She leveled her friend with a sharp stare. "Are they? I'm not sure I agree."

"Well, I'll tell you one thing." Lacey balled up her napkin and tossed it on the bar. "If that's the quality of women they're managing to pull over at MeetMyMate.com, you'd better figure it out before it's too late."

• • •

An hour later, she was at her workstation, *Seinfeld* on the TV for background noise, Lacey's words still ringing in her ears. For the first time since she bought it four years before, her tiny house felt too big. Too quiet.

Too lonely.

She opened her eyes and peered down at her cell phone again, finger paused over the call button. He was on a date. And in spite of all Cat's jealousy-fueled sniping about her,

Courtney was probably a nice person. Nicer than her, at least. She should leave them alone and let them enjoy their night together.

Night together. Overnight together? Breakfast together?

"Argh!" Cat jabbed a pin into the apricot linen dress she'd been working on. Lucky it was on a mannequin and not a model because she was pretty sure she'd have broken skin.

Maybe it doesn't have to be like this, she reminded herself for the hundredth time. If she was just willing to take a chance…

She rolled her chair back and then held the cell phone up to press call. When it rang, she bent forward until her nose almost touched her thighs hoping to quell the sudden nausea. Three rings, then four.

He wasn't going to answer.

"Hello."

Her pulse careered out of control until she realized it was only his voice mail.

"This is Shane. Leave a message, and I'll call you back."

Her stomach bottomed out and she pressed the end button, flopping backward with a groan. She'd blown it. He was still out with Courtney, and who knew, they could be exchanging bodily fluids already, and she couldn't even be mad. She'd encouraged this mess. She deserved whatever misery it caused her. Her cell vibrated in her hand, and she looked down at the screen through tear-filled eyes.

I saw you called. Something up?

Her fingers trembled over the letters, and she had to retype it twice.

Yeah. Me. Can't sleep.

His response seemed to take forever, and she wondered

where he was and what he was doing.

Sorry to hear it.

She read the abrupt response and pinched her eyes closed. What else was there to say in a text message? She'd hoped to talk to him on the phone. To explain how she was feeling, but if he couldn't take her call—

The screen lit up again.

Want me to tell you a bedtime story?

She nodded breathlessly at the phone, refusing to allow herself to think about how terrifying it was that, in the span of five seconds, he'd taken her from utter despair to total, blinding exhilaration with nothing but a text. Or how much it was going to hurt if and when this didn't work out. In fact, she didn't allow herself to think anything at all.

Her fingers flew over the touch screen.

Yes.

• • •

It didn't mean shit in the scheme of things, Shane realized. They'd danced this dance before. They'd fucked and flirted, had some near misses, and at points, he thought he'd finally gotten through to her. But he had to be realistic. If recent history was any indicator, tomorrow would come and find him right back where he'd been since their night at the hotel. Alone, frustrated, and confused.

Shane stared down at his phone, a single three-letter word staring back at him.

Yes.

He might be the world's biggest sucker, but at that moment, it was enough for him. It had to be. He typed back.

First, tell me what you're wearing. Never tell a bedtime story to a woman wearing more than one item of clothing, I always say.

He hit send and waited, wondering what she would do with that. His phone beeped a second later, and he picked it up to see the smiley-face emoticon and her reply.

A white T-shirt & a pair of long johns, but I'm taking the bottoms off right now, becuz I want my story.

Five seconds later.

K, they're off. Down to 1 article of clothing. What R U wearing?

He typed back:

Same thing you saw earlier. Jeans, sports jacket, and T-shirt.

He'd dropped Courtney off half an hour ago, and when he'd passed Cat's street, he couldn't help but drive by. Her light had been on, and he'd considered stopping by to see if she would talk to him about why she'd really shown up at Sully's. In the end, he'd stopped, but talked himself out of going up to the door, knowing he had to stick with the plan. Let her come to him.

His phone vibrated again.

Do u like her?

He considered the question and answered honestly.

She's very nice.

Does she make u laugh?

He smiled a little at that. Courtney was fun, but not like Cat, who was crazy at times but a blast to be around. Still, if this was just another game to her, he didn't want to show his whole hand.

Yes.

But even with his nifty plan in mind, it felt wrong to just leave it like that.

But not as much as you do.

Long pause, and then her reply.

I wish u were here.

That one had him shifting in his seat.

What would you do if I was?

That was the question that needed answering. Was she just jealous and confused, hoping to get his focus off Courtney, or did she really want him? His blood hummed at the thought of being inside her again. Tasting her, touching her, feeling her come against his mouth. His phone vibrated with her reply.

Whatever u asked me to.

His cock pulsed and thickened as the possibilities ran through his head like a movie. But how far to take it? What if she was just buzzed after a few beers and playing around?

R u still there?

As if he would go anywhere right now. He paused with his fingers on the keys and thought of how best to respond.

Yep. I just don't know if you're ready for what's coming out of the door you cracked open.

The wait was interminable, but when her two-word response finally came, he wanted to pound his chest and shout.

Bring it.

Maybe not a declaration of love, but pure fucking Cat Thomas. And that was enough for now.

He pressed the call button and waited. Two rings and a whispered, "Hello?"

It was past the time for games. "Are you lying down?" he demanded, his voice all grit and growl.

"I…yes. On the couch."

"Good, now take a deep breath and let it out slowly." When he heard her do it, he whispered, "Again, Cat, only this time, close your eyes. I want you to think about that night in the hotel. Remember how it felt to have my hands sliding over your body, trailing along your breasts…lower."

"Yes," she murmured.

"Spread your legs apart for me, then slide your finger along your slit. Tell me if you're wet, Cat."

A moment passed with no sound but that of her labored breathing. "Yesss."

Her response was like a fist closing over his cock, and he arched his hips helplessly toward the unseen hand.

"Don't stop. Get your fingers nice and slick and rub them over your clit. I want to hear you, babe. Tell me how it feels."

The phone was muffled for a second and then she gasped.

"Does it feel good, Cat?"

"Yes."

"You know what I remember most about that night at the lake? The sounds, those sexy little sounds you made in the back of your throat. I had blue balls for three days."

Her choked laugh made him smile.

"I don't know how I managed to walk away from you. All I can think about now is getting you to make those noises for me again."

"Wouldn't take much right now," she breathed.

His pulse thudded, and he shifted in his seat in hopes of easing the pressure in his groin. "What do you want from me, babe? Tell me and it's yours."

"Your mouth. I want your mouth on me."

Fuck yeah. "Is your clit ready for my tongue?"

"Shit, mmm, yes." Her voice was getting thicker, her words running together.

He tried to make it last, to keep talking, but his cock was like a nine iron, and his brain was starting to fry from the heat. Covering the phone with his hand, he turned off the ignition, got out of the car. He made his way to the front door almost in a daze, then turned the knob, relieved when it gave with ease. With a silent thanks to the gods of trusting cul-de-sac dwellers in low-crime Rhode Island, he pushed open the door and stepped into house. Time to see if Cat was ready to put her money where her mouth was. He padded slowly through the kitchen and stopped when he heard her whisper.

"Shane?" she murmured into the phone a little louder this time.

He stood, silent in the kitchen doorway, and stared. She was reclined on the brown leather couch, half-naked, her shapely legs bare in the moonlight. Her shirt was pushed up high to reveal peach, hard nipples standing out in stark relief against her pale skin. Her head was thrown back, red hair spread across the couch cushion, and her right hand moved delicately between her thighs. His mouth went dry, and he tried to speak in spite of all the blood draining from his brain to his cock. Only a coffee table separated them, and he fought back the urge to leap over it and pounce on her.

"Shane?" she said again, then pulled the phone away to frown at it.

"I'm here," he finally managed through gritted teeth. She jerked up and cried out.

"Holy shit, when did you—" She moved her hand from between her legs and struggled to sit up, but he crossed the room in a few short steps and stopped at the end of the couch.

"Don't stop. Put your hand back."

She stared at him, green eyes wide with shock, but the need was still there just below the surface.

"Lay back."

She hesitated for a second but slowly reclined backward, trepidation plain on her face.

"Don't be embarrassed. That was about the hottest fucking thing I've ever seen." And that was the truth. He stepped closer and took her hand, leading it back between her thighs. "You said whatever I want. This—" He slid their entwined fingers through her wet folds and his knees nearly gave out. "This is what I want."

The doubt faded, and a mischievous smile tugged at her lips. She nodded and sank deeper into the cushions. Holding his gaze in the dim light, she found her clit and fell into a hypnotic rhythm. He followed her every move as she slid her free hand up to cover one breast, caressing her nipple.

Sexy. So damned sexy.

He stripped off his coat and yanked at the button fly of his jeans. Slipping one hand down the front, he drew out his already-stiff cock and began to work it up and down in long, even strokes. She kept her eyes locked on him and her hips bounced as her hand moved faster. Too soon, her eyes drifted shut, her leg muscles tensing until Shane gripped her wrist, halting her ministrations.

"Okay. As much as I'd love to watch you for the next hour or so, that's enough. I want to be the one to make you come."

She hesitated, then lowered her gaze to his cock. She wet her lips with the tip of a pink tongue and his shaft surged in response.

"Can I taste you first?" she asked softly, reaching out a hand toward him and moving to the edge of the couch. She ran a gentle hand down his stomach, and then leaned forward to lap at the broad head of his cock. He growled low in his throat as the heat of her tongue stroked him, but it wasn't enough. He was just about to tell her so, tell her how desperate he was for her to take him deep and suck, hard, when she opened her mouth wide and worked him into her hot mouth until he felt her throat close around him in a snug embrace.

He choked out a curse and used his grip on her hair to pull her back while he tried to regain some self-control. She fought him, anchoring him to her with a grip around his thighs and using her tongue to massage him. Helpless against the onslaught, he flexed his hips restlessly, the need uncurling in his belly. She slid him almost all the way out before sucking him hard and deep again.

She met his eyes in the dim light while she sucked him off, and he wondered if he would ever forget the sight. Her head bobbing between his legs, her plump lips brushing against his cock, glossy from her mouth and tongue. He closed his eyes to block out the view because if he didn't, he was going to blow it right into her mouth and he still hadn't tasted that sweet pussy. Suddenly, that seemed to be an immediate necessity.

He pulled back, encircling her wrist to escape her grasp. She released him but ran her tongue down the length of his cock one more time for good measure.

"Nice," she whispered.

"God, you don't know how happy it makes me that you think so." He pulled away for an agonizing minute and stripped down until he was naked, then pushed her onto her back and lifted her hand high above her head.

"Lift your other arm," he ground out.

She did. And she took his breath away.

"Look at you." His gaze swept her again, and he shuddered as he nodded. "Seeing you like this, I can think of a hundred things I want to do to you, *with* you. The night at the hotel barely scratched the surface."

"You're wasting time," she said, and an instant later, he was on her. His aligned his hips against hers, her belly pressing against his cock.

He lifted his torso from her, dipping his head to take her mouth with his. Her scent enveloping, wrapping around him like a sensual blanket. He pulled back, his breathing labored as he pressed his forehead to hers.

His voice was low and hoarse. "All I can think of is you. From the second I saw you again, I wanted to slide my cock into that wet heat over and over. I want that so bad I can taste it." He slid a knee between her thighs and spread her legs open, then reached between them, covering her core with his hand. Her back bowed in response and a charge of heat blasted through him.

She let out a long hiss. "You're killing me."

He thrust himself away from her and pressed nipping kisses down her neck to her breasts, making a path to her hip. For a long moment, he just stared. When he finally dipped his head down and put his mouth to her, she nearly bucked him off, but he held her captive. He dragged his tongue over her crease, then traced around her clit with just the tip.

"Shane," she whispered urgently, arching upward.

He growled and closed his lips over the swollen knot. She shuddered and her muscles strained as she threaded her fingers into his hair, urging him to finish it. A surge of satisfaction pulsed through him and at that moment, his only purpose in life was to do it right and make her scream.

He trailed his hand along the inside of her smooth thigh

until he came close enough to feel the heat coming off her pussy. He traced her lips with his fingertips, pressing them into her wet warmth. She cried at the invasion, showing him with her body that she wanted more. He retracted, then thrust deep again, loving the feel of her, the taste of her. She thrust her hips up, grinding against his face as he increased the pressure of his mouth, sucking, licking, pulling. She froze and inner tremors racked her, squeezing him. He steeled himself for the onslaught, hoping he could keep himself from coming on the cushions like a teenager. Then she splintered under his hands, spasms taking her as she cried out his name.

Her moisture soaked his fingers. Her heat filled his mouth. Her screams filled his ears. He closed his eyes as her pussy clenched tight, tried not to imagine that it was his cock. Tried to hold it together for just a minute more.

The spasms quieted and she stilled, fighting for breath. He pushed himself onto all fours and crawled up the length of her body until they were face to face. Her cheeks were flushed, and her eyes shone.

"Nice."

He gave her a pained smile. "That's the understatement of the year." He nudged forward an inch, then two, until he could feel her slick folds. "We need a condom," he groaned, then tried to pull back.

She shook her head. "Not unless you want to. I'm on the Pill, and…it's you. It's…us."

Just like in his dreams. He pressed forward and she guided him in deep, taking his length with a shuddering sigh. He pulled back, then began the heavenly slide back in. He gritted his teeth against the sensual friction, struggling for control.

Cat reached back, snaking her hands down his back to cover his ass, then pulled him into her until he was buried to the hilt. They began to rock as one, slow and steady. He tipped his head to take a tight nipple into his mouth, and nearly exploded as her slick inner walls squeezed him in response. He matched her rhythm with long, slow, deep strokes. They moved faster, and he bent his head to lick and suck her nipple, plunging into her again and again.

"Ah, Shane!" She tightened around him like a fist, pulsing over him in waves. He squeezed his eyes shut and his cock swelled, a dull ache riding low in his balls. She went wild beneath him, rolling her hips and wriggling as she came, calling his name. She dug her nails into his back and he lost it. He pounded into her, faster and deeper until his body convulsed. He groaned her name and emptied himself into her sweet heat. In that moment, all was right in his world. If only he knew for sure that she felt the same…

Chapter Ten

Cat stared at the shadows on the wall and snuggled deeper into the covers. Shane's arm tightened around her waist, and he dragged her closer, molding her back to his front. They hadn't left each other's arms for the past five hours except to wash up, and in spite of her professed fondness for sleeping alone, she'd never felt happier. A few orgasms, a warm man in her bed...it had been a long time since that had happened. And never both at the same time until now, she realized with a chuckle.

"What's so funny?" Shane whispered, tipping his head to press a warm kiss to her shoulder.

"Oh, just thinking about self-administered orgasms and how nice it is to get them courtesy of someone else for a change."

"Well, feel free to take advantage. I've got an unlimited supply."

She pulled away then rolled in to face him. "I knew I liked you."

His face was sleepy and satisfied in the moonlight, and she

traced the dark slash of his eyebrows with her index finger. "You are one fine-looking man," she admitted. "You always were. Even when we were younger, during those rare times you took a break from torturing me, I thought you were hot."

He slung his arm over her hip and leaned in to nip at her jaw. "Did you, now? Tell me more about that. Not about the torture part. About how hot you thought I was."

She laughed and pulled away. "I did. You had to know that. The night at the lake, and…" She searched his face, debating whether she wanted to open that can of worms when things were going so nicely. But, damn it, she had to know. No point in going in with a nail file. She broke out the sledgehammer. "Why were you such an asshole to me?"

He stared at her for a long moment and then rolled away. She was just thinking maybe she should've come in a little softer when he started propping up some pillows. He settled back, flashing an exceptional expanse of muscled chest, and sighed. "I never meant to be an asshole. I was just doing what your brother asked me to do."

She leaned up onto her elbow, resisting the urge to trail her fingers over his abs. "Galen asked you to be an asshole to me?" She knew she was being thick, but she needed to know exactly what had happened that strange year, and more importantly, why Shane had walked away from her that night in the lake.

"He asked me to take care of you while he was gone. You were a little reckless, he was a lot worried, and he couldn't be there. It was your junior year. You were just coming into your own, and that body." His gaze drifted down to scan her sheet-clad form. "You had a sense of adventure and no fears. The whole thing was a like a fucking time bomb just waiting to go off. Guys that age are horny, and a lot of them are assholes. He didn't want anyone messing with you, and he didn't want you making any rash decisions you might regret later."

Understanding dawned, and she nodded slowly. "Like getting deflowered in the lake by his best friend."

"Yeah. Like that," he said with a tight smile. "Although, until now, I hadn't realized you were a virgin."

"I was. And it was all so romantic with that big moon and the warm water, it seemed like fate. You were so sweet, worried about me. You followed me in and, even when I kissed you, you hesitated. I thought it was because you didn't like me."

"Oh, I liked you. Too much." He traced the line of her shoulder and frowned. "Jesus, how could you not have known that? I was hard as a baseball bat and breathing like I just went ten rounds with a grizzly."

She chuckled. "I knew you wanted me, same as any teenage boy naked in a lake with a girl. I didn't know you liked me, though. You were always treating me like a sister, dragging me out of places and embarrassing me."

"Never my intention. I was doing what I promised your brother I would do. Believe me, it wasn't easy. I thought about it every minute for a year afterward, and at least once a day since."

The admissions sent a thrill through her, and she wriggled closer. "Well, it so happens that I still think you're pretty fine."

"Thank you, ma'am. You're pretty fine yourself. In fact"—he closed a hand over her hip and squeezed—"if you're not busy for the next hour or so, I'd like to spend it making up for that night."

She pressed closer to him. "Sounds good," she whispered.

"I can't give you the lake and the moon, but you do have that big bathtub, and we can leave the light on," he said with a brow waggle.

She laughed and rolled away. "Meet you there!" She stood, buck naked, making an effort not to run, in spite of her nerves…to take it slow so that he could enjoy the view.

He groaned and let out a pained laugh. "My kingdom for a camera."

She made it to the door and faced him. "You should bring us a couple ice waters. And maybe a snack. This is going to take a while." She shut the door behind her and leaned against it. Why it was such a relief that Shane had suffered as much as she had that night, she couldn't say. Maybe misery really did love company. Or maybe she was just a bad person. Either way, she felt a lightness and a confidence she hadn't felt in years.

She crossed the long room and set a towel on the edge of the chilly white porcelain. The giant, claw-footed tub had been one of her favorite features of the house, and she'd made use of it many times over the past few years, but never with a man. Never with Shane.

She turned the water on hot and sat on the edge of the tub, waiting for it to fill. It was only halfway when he stepped into the room, arms laden with bottled water and a plate piled high with what looked like peanut butter sandwiches. She nearly snort-laughed. "You bypassed the strawberries and cheese in the fridge for peanut butter?"

"Peanut butter and *Fluff*. I didn't want to be cliché. Plus," he said, setting the food on the sink and giving her a slow wink, "we might need the protein."

Despite his teasing words, the look of naked desire on his face make her heart kick double-time, and she reached for him, tugging his hips closer to line up with her face. "Seems like somebody is already prepped for game time," she murmured, tugging his boxers down to release his swollen shaft. It bounced and settled high on his belly and she wet her lips. Big strong man, big and strong everywhere.

He hummed low in his throat and his response came on a growl. "He's been waiting for some water sex with you for almost ten years."

She tipped her head closer, shifting on her perch to get close enough for a long, slow lick.

"Ah, fuck," he groaned, tunneling a hand into her hair. She curled her fingers around his thick shaft and drew it down to flick the head with her tongue. His fingers tensed and the tug at her scalp made her smile.

"I think he likes me," she whispered, making sure her warm breath washed over the length of him. She reveled in the warm, musky taste of him and went back for another long lick.

He cursed and stepped in, bringing himself more fully into her mouth, and she took him without hesitation. Steam curled around them, enveloping them in a warmth that settled over her and bloomed in her center as she sucked. She worked her throat muscles to draw him deeper, his whispered broken words of praise urging her on. Power and desire pulsed through her, and her clit ached with need. She played her lips and tongue over the satin-encased steel until he jerked away, legs quivering. His cock pulsed as his harsh breathing echoed through the room.

"Get in the tub, Cat," he demanded, closing a hand over his cock and fisting himself as she stood. As desperate as she was to move forward, she couldn't take her eyes off him, cupping his heavy balls before stroking up the girth of his shaft, milking himself.

"Do you like to watch me?"

She nodded wordlessly.

"Would you like to watch me come like this? I could, so easily. Especially with you looking at me like that. Like the other night. When you were on your back, those gorgeous tits ready, nipples hard." The chords in his neck stood out and his voice was all grit, his hand moving faster.

She stared down, mesmerized by the bead of moisture that had escaped the head of his cock. She reached out her hand, and he stilled, his breath choppy and uneven. "But not today. Turn off the tub, Cat, and get in. Now."

The sharp command should have annoyed her. Instead it sent a bolt of lightning through her that settled between her thighs, and she found herself complying without hesitation.

"Don't forget your knee," he added, more softly this time. "It's going to sting, so take it slow."

Emotion clogged her throat. The lightning, or at least a paler form of it, she'd felt before. The sense of being cared for like that? Never. And damn if she didn't like the combination.

She slipped into the tub with a sigh, the hot water caressing her toes, ankles, and calves until she sank down, immersing herself. The knee did sting, but the bliss of the water working over her tired muscles was heaven. Shane had given her a workout earlier.

"Slide toward the center so I can get in behind you," he murmured.

She did and he stepped in to settle behind her, his thighs cradling her hips. The water sloshed to the edge of the tub and over, but she didn't care. The feel of him, hot and hard against her back, was sublime.

He slid his arms around her waist and pulled her tighter to him, his thick cock branding her back.

"Nice," she hissed, wishing she was facing him so her good parts lined up with his.

He kissed the top of her head. "It's about to get even nicer." He released her to trace a winding path over her rib cage beneath the water, gliding closer to the underside of her breasts with each pass. "Your skin is incredible."

The tub squeaked as she shifted lower, trying to rush him, hoping to get him to cup her breasts. To pinch her aching nipples. Another slide and his thumb just narrowly missed one. She groaned in frustration as the bead tightened further, pouting for attention. "Touch me, Shane."

"I *am* touching you, Mary Catherine. Just not where you want right now." His voice was hypnotic and she stilled. He was going to do this his way, and the sooner she let him, the sooner he'd put her out of her sweet misery and reward her with a mind-blowing orgasm.

"Fine. Do your worst."

He tossed his head back and laughed, his chest shaking against her back. "Such a martyr. I'm not trying to torture you like I used to, you know. This is just as hard on me." He flexed his hips into the small of her back. "Harder, even. But tonight I'm determined to do the things I never got to at the lake."

His fingertips skimmed over the swells of her breasts and again narrowly missed the stiff tips.

"Drape your legs over mine."

She did. Her nipples grew impossibly tight, the heat of his gaze from over her shoulder setting her aflame. His hands abandoned her breasts, but before she could miss them, one was cupped over her stomach, the other cradling her pubic bone.

"You had on peach underwear," he whispered, grinding the heel of his palm in exactly the right spot. "They were just cotton, boy-cut panties but I swear to God, they were sexier on you than any Victoria's Secret thong I've ever seen. The bra matched. Sort of. Except for the tiny green polka dots."

The hand on her stomach traveled up, covering her breast, and she arched into him.

"I wanted to trace every one of them with the tip of my tongue. Do you know I've had a polka dot fetish ever since?" His low laugh held more passion than humor. "You were a fucking dream."

His words were as seductive as his hands and she tried to twist around in his arms. "I want…you inside me, Shane. Please."

But he held her still, continuing the delicious torture.

"When you stepped into the water and tossed that look at me over your shoulder, all sass and dare, with that sweet ass peeking out the bottom of those underwear, a school of piranha couldn't have stopped me."

"P-piranhas only live in the Amazon," she murmured, not caring that it sounded inane.

"I couldn't help but wonder what was under there. A thatch of red curls? A sleek strip of rust? Now I know. So neat, and sweet." She stared down between her thighs, mesmerized by his fingers, sliding over the smattering of strawberry hair and deeper, to part her folds.

"Ah, Jesus," she whimpered, gnawing her bottom lip as his fingers found her clit.

"Did you touch yourself that night, Mary Catherine?" She didn't answer, sensation swamping her senses to the point that she didn't trust herself to speak.

"Did you make yourself come thinking of me grinding against you in the warm water? Fuck knows, I did. I jerked off when I got home and came so hard, I thought my head was going to blow off."

His clever fingers moved faster now, circling her clit in a rhythm that made her throat ache from holding back a scream. "Nothing stopping us now, babe." He curled his hand, sending two fingers deep, and she shuddered.

He grunted and froze. "So wet. Jesus, Cat. Stand up. I want to take you from behind so I can see us. See that sweet ass while I fuck you."

The need she'd thought couldn't possibly get stronger doubled up in a rush. She stood and flipped on the shower. He rose behind her and pressed his palm against the center of her back, urging her to bend at the waist. She propped her hands on the slick gray tile, and dipped lower. The feel of his hot gaze encouraged her to take her time, pose a little for him. He must have liked the view because he let out a muffled groan.

She gave her bottom a wiggle and peered over her shoulder to see his gaze locked on her.

"What are you waiting for?"

He shook his head as if to clear it. "Hell if I know," he said with a pained smile. He closed his big, strong hands over her ass. He spread her wide, pressing his thumbs into the delicate tissue between her cheeks, and she moaned.

"That sound is making me nuts. I want to take it slow, but I need you so bad right now." His voice was harsh, as if he'd walked miles in the desert without a sip of water. All she wanted to do was slake his thirst.

"I don't want it slow. Don't make me wait, Shane," she pleaded.

He bit out a curse and then his hands slipped lower, massaging her from behind, spreading her wide. The thick head of his cock probed her slit, up and down, spreading her slick juices around her overheated flesh. Unable to take any more teasing, she flexed back against him, taking him deep. He tipped his hips forward until he was flush against her. For a moment, she forgot to breathe. The fullness was a double-edged sword. It was so sublime she almost wept, but at the same time it was torturous, turning want into a blaze of white-hot need.

"Please," she whispered.

He didn't answer, choosing to respond with his body. He pulled back, then arched forward, filling her again in an erotic slide. He repeated the motion, working in and out in slow, measured thrusts. She scrabbled at the tile, her hands like talons as he took her higher, luring her closer to the precipice. He rode her hard, with deep, steady strokes that curled her toes. He shifted, pushing her forward until every lunge ground the root of his cock hard against her aching clit. The sensation roared through her, like a train at full speed.

"I'm going to come," she groaned.

He encouraged her with murmured words, quickening his pace until the wave slammed into her, wrecking her. Her body felt as if it were made of light as the tremors shook her. She dimly heard him calling her name.

"That's it. God, so tight." On a shout, he tumbled after her. His cock pulsed deep inside her, and she held on as his body shook behind hers.

Pure satisfaction coursed through her when he leaned forward, draping his torso over her back. His heart beat a rapid tattoo against her spine, and she smiled.

When they were both able to breathe, he pulled away. He flipped off the shower and reached for her, scooping her in his arms.

She squealed, laughing as he carried her into the bedroom. "We're soaking wet, and that's a four-hundred-dollar silk comforter! Don't even think of dropping me on that."

He set her gently on the floor and went back into the bathroom, returning with some towels a few seconds later. "Dry off while I go get our forgotten snacks."

Ten minutes later, replete with her lunchbox sandwich and great sex, she slipped back into the bed. "Delicious," she groaned with a satisfied stretch. And it was. She replayed the night in her mind and shivered. Had she really thought of him as boring? God, she couldn't have been more wrong.

He settled in behind her and wrapped his arm around her waist. "I'm glad you liked it."

She traced his muscled forearm and marveled at how happy and settled she felt. The usual urge to run away was nowhere to be found. In fact, she wanted nothing more than to snuggle in tighter and sleep in his arms. Maybe this could work, after all. Just maybe…

Her mind wandered, fantasies of them vacationing on a tropical island and skiing together in Vermont ran through her head.

"Do you scuba dive?" she asked.

No response.

"Shane?"

She turned to look at him and realized he was dead asleep. His deep, even breaths—almost like a soft snore—had her grinning. They could talk tomorrow. She'd grill him about his date with Courtney and see if maybe he'd consider putting a hold on his MeetMyMate.com membership until they had a chance to explore this thing between them.

Thing? It's love, you idiot.

The unbidden thought sent her pulse racing with terror, and she waited for the need to flee. But it never came. Was it possible that she'd found a man who was worth risking it for? A man who knew exactly who she was and who wasn't intimidated by it? There was no way to know for sure, but for the first time in her life, she found herself wanting to see if this could go somewhere. If they could stick. She tucked in tighter, making herself the little spoon. Tomorrow, she would make Lacey proud and open up to a man for the first time in her life.

She closed her eyes and drifted off to sleep, visions of Shane in her head.

Chapter Eleven

Light streamed through the window, and Shane cursed under his breath at a persistent buzzing noise.

"Are you going to get that?" Cat's muffled voice came from beneath a mountain of blankets, and he grinned. She was curled into a ball and almost invisible, with only a few rusty curls poking out from the top of her makeshift fort.

"Yeah, I was dead to the world. Didn't even realize it was my phone." He lifted the covers and gave her bare bottom a pat before rolling off the bed. He'd barely taken a step when he tripped over the mound of clothes littering the beige carpet. "Don't you have a closet for this stuff?"

"Doesn't all fit."

He pushed the pile aside with his foot and glanced at the clock. Almost 9:00 a.m. The last time he'd slept that late had been in college. By the time he found his jeans and dug his phone out of his pocket, the call had gone to voice mail. Good. With Cat still warm and sleepy, maybe he could—

The phone buzzed in his hand and he bit back a curse. He peered down at the number. Galen. He spared a glance at Cat and held up a finger. His buddy was on board with the idea of them dating, but he probably didn't need to know that Shane had spent the night.

"Hello?"

"Hey, it's Galen." His friend's voice sounded strange, and Shane tensed instantly.

"What's going on, man?"

"Lacey and I are on our way to New York City for the weekend, but Rafe asked me to give you a call when I told him you were in town." If Galen's tone had been strained before, it was even more so now. "Shit, man, there's a child missing in Caseville. Grace Abbott, four years old. The Abbotts have a cottage on Elmer Lake. They need volunteers, like now."

Shane's stomach clenched. Kids missing near lakes were always scary.

"They went to bed last night, kids tucked in and all was well," Galen continued. "This morning, they woke around seven-thirty when they felt a draft coming from under their bedroom door. Gracie was gone and the front door was wide open. The PD is already on the scene, and Rafe is putting together a search party. He asked if you could make it over there to help."

Shane stalked to the window and shoved the curtains aside. Fat flakes of snow fell to the already-covered ground. *Fuck.* He speared a hand through his hair and started running scenarios in his head. They went from bad to unthinkable, depending on how small the child was, what she'd been wearing, and what the temperature was when she left the house. Had someone taken her? Had she seen something out her window and gone to explore? Maybe she'd managed to find shelter somewhere and was huddled up with a stuffed animal or her favorite blanket. He refused to even think about the lake.

Shane juggled the phone and dragged his jeans on. "Are

there signs of an abduction?"

"Shane? What's going on?" Cat sat up on the bed, her face drained of color.

He covered the receiver and explained quickly. "There's a missing girl in Caseville. I'm going to join the search party to help find her." He turned his attention back to Galen on the telephone.

"They said that kidnapping looks unlikely at this point. Only one tiny set of prints in the snow leading from the house into the woods. Unfortunately, they get sporadic from there once the canopy of evergreens shields large sections of the forest floor."

"Okay, give Rafe a call back and tell him I'll be there ASAP."

Cat stood, wrapping a sheet around her and started for the bathroom. "I'm coming, too. I want to help."

He relayed that to Galen who, to his credit, didn't ask why he was with Cat so early in the morning. "They have five guys from the precinct there now," Galen said, "but the rest of the volunteers are neighbors and family, so I know they'll appreciate your expertise."

He gave Shane the address and they disconnected. By the time he got his socks and shoes on, Cat was coming out of the bathroom fully dressed.

"Make sure you put on snow boots."

"What about you?" she asked, peering down at the dress shoes he'd worn for his date the night before.

"No time. I'll be fine."

She looked like she wanted to argue but then nodded. "Let's go."

The twenty-minute ride felt like an eternity, and in spite of her efforts to fill the heavy silence, he could feel the rising tension between them. He wished he knew why, or how to stop it, but right now, every ounce of his energy needed to be focused on Grace Abbott. *Gracie*, Galen had called her.

Gracie, whom they would find alive and well.

"It's this left," Cat said, pointing to a narrow, snow-covered road marked Pawtuck 7-15.

He made the turn and pulled up to the small house where a dozen people stood in a half-circle around Rafe, who was handing out sheets of paper.

He and Cat exited the car and approached the group.

"Thanks for coming, guys, much appreciated." Rafe gestured for Shane to stand next to him, and Cat moved to line up with the other civilian volunteers.

Shane scanned the group, taking in the expectant faces pinched with worry. His old friend continued in an authoritative, steady tone. "This is Shane Decker. Shane is a specialist and has traveled all over the world developing search-and-rescue procedures for government and private organizations alike, as well as spearheading rescues for countless global disasters. We're very lucky to have him here today to help us find little Gracie."

He turned to Shane and handed him a map. "We have one group out now—ten people including the parents—with our field officers, and a three-man crew of park rangers from the fish and game department. They're focusing on the perimeter of the lake."

The group was dressed appropriately, thank God, and seemed highly motivated and ready to listen. He took a long look at the map before addressing them.

"That's a good start," Shane said with a nod. "If she's already gotten to a main road, which seems unlikely, there's a better chance of her being found or seen. So, for now, we're going to start with the three square miles of wooded terrain surrounding the house. If we work in ever-widening circles around the lake rather than taking a few square acres at a time, we'll form a virtual net of eyes and ears. That way, if she's still on the move, it will minimize the chance of her always being one section ahead of or behind us."

The volunteers murmured and nodded.

Several officers exited the cottage, and an older woman followed to stand on the porch. Her arms were crossed over her chest tight, and her face was a mask of grief.

Rafe followed his line of sight and pursed his lips. "That's the grandmother, Maggie Abbott. She's not in the best of health but wanted to come and help. She's going to stay at the house and wait in case Grace finds her way back."

"Cat, can you go with Maggie and see if the two of you can set up a hot drink and food station for the team? It could be a while and in these temperatures, people are going to have to rest, warm up, and refuel. Maybe also see if you can dig up spare sets of gloves, hats, and scarves in case things get wet or lost?"

Cat's eyes narrowed, but she nodded briskly and crunched through the snow toward Maggie. He watched her receding back, saying one more silent prayer for Gracie. He'd sent Cat to be with the grandmother partly for the reason he'd said, and partly because Maggie Abbott clearly needed a strong shoulder. But if he was being honest with himself, there was a far bigger reason.

He scanned the volunteers and swallowed the bile that rose in his throat. One of these people would find Gracie. He knew it as sure as he knew his own name because he wouldn't sleep until they did. What he didn't know was whether she would be alive or dead.

Sometimes he fucking hated this job.

"Okay, team. Here's how we're going to do it."

• • •

Cat stared out the window while stirring the pot of hot

chocolate on the stove. It had been three hours, and soon, another major storm was set to pass through. The teams had made a full pass through the woods to no avail, aside from a tiny red boot that had been found on one of the trails an hour before. Shane had doubled the number of people searching that area, but so far, they hadn't heard any news.

"We've got four coming in right now," Maggie called from the front door.

Cat ran over to stand next to her, trying to make out the silhouettes in the distance. No Shane. He had only come in once since they'd arrived, and that had only been to fill a thermos full of coffee and go back out. She tamped down the worry, reminding herself for the hundredth time that he was the expert. He'd know when it was time to take a break. She went back into the kitchen to ladle up four steaming mugs of cocoa and then set them on the table.

Maggie bustled in a moment later and grabbed a log from the woodpile near the door. "I'm going to build up the fire a bit."

Cat nodded. "Good idea." She watched Maggie struggle with the log through the doorway to the living room, but knew better than to offer to help. Somehow, right from the get-go, Shane had known that Maggie needed a job to do, and had Cat give her one that she was taking very seriously. In the midst of this horrifying, chaotic event in her life, he'd given her a purpose, and Cat was fairly certain that purpose was the only thing holding the older woman together right now.

She glanced at the clock again and bit her lip. Maggie wasn't the only one having a hard time keeping it together. In the hours since Gracie's disappearance, Cat had met her parents, seen the wear on their faces, watched friends and family file in and out, getting more despondent with every passing hour. She'd listened to Maggie tell story after story about her "little love bug." The first time Gracie had said "grandma," which came out more like "gamma" and had stuck to this day. The way she loved to play tea party with her dolls, only instead of tea, they had soup because tea was yucky.

As the day progressed and the stories got too hard to tell, Maggie would disappear for a while and Cat would pace around the small cottage, trying not to look at the family photos plastering the walls, slowly driving her insane. Gracie as a chubby toddler in her swimmies on the pier. Gracie on Christmas morning surrounded by gifts, doe-like brown eyes full of wonder. Gracie in her little blue coat by the lake feeding the ducks.

Cat squeezed the bridge of her nose and swallowed hard.

"You okay?"

She dashed the tears from her eyes and turned to find Rafe standing by the table cupping a mug of cocoa in a gloved hand. She hadn't even heard him come in.

"Yeah, I'm good. Fine. You?"

He nodded grimly. "Yeah. Just fine."

Neither of them was fine. She needed only to look at the tightness around his mouth and feel the mounting sense of hopelessness hanging between them, unspoken, to know it.

She cleared her throat to dislodge the lump that had wedged itself there. "It's getting really cold out there. Maybe I should spell one of the search party members who've been out all day and someone can come in here? The parents haven't stopped since this morning." She wrapped her arms around her shoulders to chase away the shiver that went through her every time she thought of little Gracie out there in the cold for more than five hours.

Rafe shrugged and looked away. "The Abbotts won't come in until Gracie's been found. The rest of the crew is dressed for the weather, and it's stopped snowing, so overall, not too bad as far as cold goes. Plus, you're doing a great job and I think it's better for Maggie if you're here now that you have a rapport."

"Whatever you think is best." She wasn't about to argue with him. She only wanted to help. Still, something in his face—

Frantic shouts from outside and Rafe's suddenly beeping radio urged them to rush to the front door. Cat's heart pounded in her chest when they stepped onto the porch and scanned the yard. Three adult silhouettes ran through the snowy woods in the distance, the largest cradling a small, motionless figure.

"Oh sweet Jesus." Maggie stood in the doorway, face drained of color. "Please, God, please no."

The shouts grew louder and moving shapes became clearer. Shane. It was Shane, and he had Gracie in his arms wrapped in a blanket, one red boot sticking out of the bottom.

One of the three, a female volunteer, broke away, sprinting toward the house. Tears streamed unchecked down her face. "She's alive, she's going to be okay!"

Maggie let out a sob and rushed down the stairs. Rafe followed after her, taking her arm to help her traverse the snowy ground. Cat looked on from the porch, gripping the railing like a lifeline, as Shane strode up to the child's grandmother and lifted the blanket away from Gracie's face.

"She's exhausted. Still dehydrated and won't drink much. She's got a moderate case of hypothermia, but I saw no signs of frostbite. An ambulance will be here in five minutes or less to take her to the hospital and have her checked out."

Maggie dropped her head onto Gracie's chest. "Thank you, thank you," she murmured over and over, wrapping her arms around her granddaughter and the man who had brought her home.

"Did someone notify the parents yet?" Rafe asked.

Shane nodded, pulling away from Maggie. "Yes. We called

them, and they're en route now. They were about a mile out, so they'll be here any minute. Maggie," he said gently, "let's get her inside near the fire until the ambulance comes, all right?"

Maggie straightened and took a shuddering breath. "Of course, of course, come on."

She gripped Shane's elbow like she couldn't bear to lose contact and led them up the stairs to where Cat stood looking on. He searched her face. "You okay?"

She pasted on a reassuring smile. "I'm great." But that was a lie. She peered down at Grace's face, pink and so very alive, and her relief was so all-encompassing that her legs could barely hold her. She was a nanosecond away from breaking into gut-wrenching sobs, but managed to hold it together through sheer force of will. She followed them into the house, joined by the rescue crews and police officers who had begun trickling in from the woods.

The chatter was jubilant and incessant coming from all directions, but Cat was able to piece together that Gracie had heard a noise outside in the wee hours of the morning and hoped it was Santa coming again. She'd donned her boots and went outside to follow the sounds but, with the snow falling, had quickly gotten lost. At some point, she came across a ground-level wooden hunting blind about a mile from the cottage. She went inside, burrowed beneath an old wool blanket she found on the floor, and fell asleep. One of the volunteers had passed the blind and even approached to look inside, but didn't see the tiny girl under the dirty old blanket. Luckily, when Shane heard about the boot being found, he went back to the area and saw the blind as well.

"Thank you for coming with me." Shane had come up behind her and laid a hand on her shoulder. "You did a really great job holding Maggie together."

"Thanks." She turned to face him, barely resisting the

urge to trace the lines of tension bracketing his mouth. "It's okay now. You did it. She's home."

"Yeah. And I'm very relieved. It just...brings back memories of the times that didn't turn out as well." His intense eyes grew dark, and she wanted to comfort him, but felt so fragile herself that if she did they might both fall apart. She needed to get out of this place, and fast. Go home, cry it out. Burrow under a blanket herself until she could face the world again.

The sound of a siren wailed in the distance. "We should go, let the family take care of her now," Shane said, jutting his chin toward the door.

"Sounds like a good idea."

She followed him to the closet for her coat, where they were met by Rafe. He put a hand on Shane's shoulder. "You were a lifesaver today, man. Literally. I appreciate you coming out."

"Your team is great. You guys would have found her without me, but I'm glad I was here to help."

Rafe shook his head. "I don't know if that's true, but thanks for saying so. I'd like to talk to you about some training in the future, when you're back for good and settled in."

"Sounds like a plan."

By tacit agreement, she and Shane slipped out without saying good-bye to the Abbotts. Their full attention needed to be on Gracie right now.

By the time they got to the truck, the adrenaline that had been sustaining her drained from her body, leaving her exhausted.

"I didn't even do anything, and I feel like I need to sleep for a week." She wrapped her arms around her shoulders and shivered, the cold seeming to penetrate into her very bones.

"You did plenty," he assured her, tugging his gloves off and setting them on the console between them. They were wet, and his hands were bone white. She took one in hers and gasped.

"Jesus, your hands are like ice and your gloves are wet. Can you even feel your fingers? And your feet must be soaked through."

He pulled away from her and got his keys from his pocket to start the engine. "I'm fine," he insisted. "I've been way colder than this before."

Anger sent a welcome blast of heat and energy through her. "Is that supposed to make me feel better? You could have gotten frostbite. Why didn't you come in for a break to warm up and get some dry gloves and socks, at least?"

He sighed and pulled the truck from the driveway. "Time wasn't on our side. We needed one crew to continue the sweep so we could make sure to get the whole area again before the next storm, and we needed another to focus on the area around the boot. It was more important for the people less accustomed to the prolonged cold to take breaks, and I didn't want to leave either crew shorthanded."

"If you needed more bodies out there, why didn't you let me come out to help? I asked Rafe, and he—"

Shane's face went notably blank, and his fingers clenched the wheel more tightly, sending a trickle of dread down her spine.

"Tell me you didn't convince Rafe to keep me inside because you didn't want my dainty little self to catch a chill." If the air was cold, her tone was arctic.

He turned the heat on without a word and it blasted tepid air.

At his telling lack of response, all the emotion that had been simmering just beneath the surface erupted in a snarl. "Who the hell do you think you are?"

Chapter Twelve

Shane kept his eyes on the snowy back road, but he didn't need to see her to know she was beyond furious. He did a perfunctory soul-searching but couldn't find even a morsel of regret for his actions, so she was shit out of luck if she expected an apology.

"It wasn't just the cold, Cat." He tried to keep the emotion from his voice and stated the facts, hoping she would understand, but resigning himself to the consequences if she didn't. He wasn't going to lie to her no matter how much the truth pissed her off. "I didn't want you to find her."

The words hung in the air between them until she started to sputter. "I don't understand. You like being a hero so much that you didn't want to miss out on the glory? If that's the case, then I don't even know who you are."

Her lack of faith in his character cut deep, but he didn't let it show. Emotions were high; it had been a rough day on everyone. "Obviously not. And maybe I phrased that incorrectly. What I meant was that I didn't want you to find her because I didn't think she was going to be found alive."

He gave her a second to process what he was saying, then continued. "It's freezing, we didn't know how long she'd been out or if she'd managed to find shelter. Jesus, Cat, we're right next to a huge lake. Do you have any idea what it's like to see a child who's drowned?" He shook his head and tried to block out the memories of a recent monsoon rescue effort. "I come in with a can-do attitude with every job, but if I had to put a number on it? Gracie's chances were less than fifty percent and dropping with every hour. If she hadn't made it… Seeing something like that weighs on you."

He gritted his teeth against the twinge of guilt that crept in. "I care about you too much to watch you go through that. We needed someone inside to help Maggie and keep the teams nourished and warm. You were as good a choice as anyone."

"Her parents were out there," she argued, fists balled on her thighs.

"That wasn't my call. If there had been something I could do to dissuade them, believe me, I would have. You didn't need to be there. And face it, you did help, Cat. Maggie needed someone badly, and I know the team appreciated everything you did. I don't think some of them would have been able to stay out as long as they did if not for you guys keeping them going with the coffee and dry gear."

She was quiet for so long, he wondered if she was going to respond at all. Then she blew out a weary sigh and slumped deeper into the seat. "I thought we were past this. I thought you'd accepted that I don't want a guy who feels like he needs to take care of me. I can take care of myself."

There was no anger now, which should have been a good sign, but somehow the resignation and sadness in her voice was far more chilling.

"Just take me home, Shane."

For the rest of the ride, they didn't speak, but he could

feel her fortifying the wall between them, brick by brick. He thought about pressing her, pushing for a resolution, but he'd used the last reserves of his energy back in the woods, and neither one of them was in a good frame of mind for a conversation. By the time they pulled into her driveway, he wondered if she'd drifted off.

"Did you want to come in for a minute? I can make you a hot coffee to go, and I'm sure I can find a dry pair of socks to fit you." The offer was clipped, delivered in much the same way a DMV employee might ask an impatient driver to take a number, and forced him to reconsider putting off the rest of their conversation.

He turned to face her. "Look, I know you're mad at me right now, but let's not leave things like this. I need you to understand that I wasn't trying to hurt you back there."

"The thing is, I'm not even mad. I *was* mad. Now I'm just like…whatever." She angled toward him and took his still-chilly hand in her gloved one. "This wasn't your fault. You're a hero, and you saved that little girl's life today. I think you're an amazing person, and I let that sway me. I always knew we weren't right for each other."

"Come on, Cat. I just wanted to protect you."

"That's the problem. I don't need protecting." Her green gaze was clear with resolve. "You think because you kept me from choking or bandaged my knee that I need you to take care of me all the time? I hate to break it to you, but I wouldn't have needed saving if you hadn't been there fucking my head all up. And I don't want the man in my life assuming he knows what's best for me. I need a companion who wants to have dinner followed by some good sex, then sort of do our own thing so I can get back to taking over the world, solo. That's not you, Shane."

She jabbed a finger in his direction, her voice breaking. "You fill up the room, even the corners, until there's no space for anything else. When I'm with you, I can't think of anything else. It's a short trip from there to me staying home knitting booties for fun instead of skating roller derby. I'm terrified that I'll start to like your protection, and I'll wake up some day to find my bucket list, wrinkled and yellow, stuffed in the back of a drawer next to my dusty nunchucks. Trust me, it's better that we realized it now before there's nothing left but resentment and regret."

He could feel his jaw tense and again considered trying to stay this discussion until the next day, but he couldn't help himself. "That's bullshit."

She drew back, a little of the fire back in her eye. "Really? And what's bullshit about it? It's always been this way, even when we were young."

"I'm so sick of you throwing that in my face. Do you have any idea how hard that was on me? I wanted you so badly, it was all I could think about. But I made a promise to your brother that I would watch out for you. I keep my promises. Always."

"Fine then, you want to tell yourself that's all it is? Fast-forward to present tense. We've slept with each other twice and you're already squashing me again. I'd say that's a pretty good indicator of things to come."

He let out a snort of disgust. "You can downplay it all you want, but we're not two strangers who banged after a night at the bar a couple of times. I know you have feelings for me and I sure as shit have feelings for you, which is why I didn't want to see you hurt. It's called caring about someone."

She jerked her head around to gaze out the side window, but he wasn't having it. "Fucking look at me," he growled.

She turned to face him again, teeth clenched.

"I'd never ask you to give up doing the things you love or to stop crossing things off your bucket list. Those are the things that make you *you*. I just wanted to shield you from some pain. Is that so wrong?"

She didn't roll her eyes, but she didn't need to. Her hand was on the door handle, and she was clearly mentally checking out of this conversation. He yanked off his seat belt and pulled at his coat zipper.

"What are you doing?" she asked with a frown.

He struggled out of his coat sleeves and then pulled his shirt over his head. He jabbed a finger at the symbol tattooed on his shoulder. "I got this last year, to commemorate five years on the job. Five years of triumphs. Five years of failures, and believe me, those stick with you." A familiar pain welled up as he remembered some of the tougher ones, but he pushed past it. "I'd rather cut off my own arm than have you go through that. The thing is? My job also makes me realize how precious life is. That's what made me want to come home and be with family."

A fat tear dripped down her cheek to her mouth, and she licked it away.

"And that's what makes me a hundred percent sure that being with someone you love is worth fighting for, no matter the risks." He took her hand and squeezed it, but she pulled away.

"Where is this talk about love coming from?"

Her voice had gone shrill and her eyes wild. He knew that look. Cat prepping to run for it. "If I hadn't been drinking that night, we wouldn't even be here right now," she said. "All we know is that we're sexually compatible. Nothing else. I've been doing a lot of things that make it seem otherwise, but I'm being one hundred percent real with you right now." She pulled the door handle and it swung open, letting in a blast of cold. "I don't want to be in a relationship like this. I don't want to be a wife. I don't want to be a mother. I don't *want* to want this. This has got to stop, or I'm going to lose my mind. Just because we have great chemistry doesn't mean we'd make a great couple." She unlatched her seat belt and started to get out of the truck.

Anger burned in the pit of his gut and he let it rip. "You said that before, you know. That night in Atlantic City. Like you think this was some spur-of-the-moment thing for me. Like you fucked me right that first night, and now I'm pussy-whipped and decided we should be together forever."

She ignored him, scrambling desperately to gather her stuff from the floor, but he pressed on.

"That's so far from the truth. I came back here for you, Cat. Because I've always known we'd make a great couple. Since we were teenagers. I was just waiting for you to grow up and realize it, too."

She was already out the door when he called after her.

"My mistake was thinking you ever would."

Chapter Thirteen

Cat revved the snowmobile hard and gave Galen a gloved thumbs-up when he looked back to see if she was set to go. She was more than ready for their trek up the little mountain. Maybe it would clear her head. Nothing else had lately. Hell, who was she kidding? The only thing that could clear her head today would be a lobotomy. Because today? Today, Shane was going back to California.

An ache settled in her chest, so heavy it took her breath away.

She'd found out the day before, entirely by accident, when she'd run into his mother at the grocery store. Lacey had seen him over the past two weeks, but according to her friend, Shane hadn't said a word about leaving. Maybe he hadn't wanted to explain to anyone why he'd had a change of heart, but she knew why.

She swallowed the lump in her throat that seemed almost constant lately. Every time she thought of him, she found herself close to tears.

She watched dispassionately as her brother shot forward,

heading up the gleaming white hill. Hitting the gas, she lurched forward and started at a steady clip a short distance behind him. The sun glinted off the hard-packed snow and made the whole place shimmer like it had been frosted in crushed diamonds.

But even the stunning view barely penetrated the fog of despair.

This was the first time she'd left her house except to go to work since she'd seen Shane last. She was already two weeks behind on her designs, and if she didn't get some inspiration and start producing soon, she was going to be in serious trouble. Everything seemed just a little less important now than it had before, and she wondered what would happen if she didn't turn in her pieces. And forget checking things off her bucket list. All the adventures she'd planned over the rest of her vacation had paled in comparison to the reality of being with Shane.

It was those kinds of observations that had Lacey clucking around her like a mother hen. Cat could tell how relieved her friend had been when she'd agreed to this outing. She seemed hopeful that it signaled that Cat was coming out of her funk, but in fact, placating Lacey and Galen had really been the only reason Cat had gone.

Shit was so far from okay.

Still, she vowed to squeeze some peace out of the day. Lacey had stayed behind at the Thomas lake house and was working on a chicken potpie for their lunch. It had been years since they'd gone snowmobiling, and at the very least, maybe she could turn her brain off for a while and not hurt for a change. No matter how much she wanted to be with Shane, it didn't change the fact that eventually, she'd wind up resenting him if she allowed him to change her.

She'd slowed down some while she'd been thinking, and now sped up to close the distance between her and Galen, needing the speed and the icy air stinging her cheeks.

She'd just taken a tight corner when a white rabbit shot out in front of her. Her heart leaped from her chest and, instinctively, she jerked the handlebars hard to the right to avoid it. She recognized her mistake instantly, but it was too late. The pine stump loomed as she plowed toward it, almost in slow motion. The impact shook every bone in her body, and then she was airborne. Over the handlebars, flying. Her arms pinwheeled and she scrambled for purchase, but the ground came up fast. She braced herself, covering her head with her arms.

She landed a like a sack of stones a dozen feet away and nausea swept over her. Her ears buzzed like a thousand bees were descending. Dimly, she heard the growl of the other engine coming closer. Galen would flip if he saw her like this. She rolled to her side and tried to stand, to let him know she was okay, but a shooting pain raced up her leg and she fell back in a crumpled heap.

Well, shit.

An hour and a half later, after a humiliating ride back to the cottage on the back of Galen's snowmobile, she lay sprawled on a hospital bed in a paper-thin gown, waiting for the ER doctor to come back with her X-ray results. Truth was, she didn't need any results to tell her she'd broken her ankle. Again.

The ache was persistent, and the antiseptic smell of the room was making her nauseous. She closed her eyes in an attempt to meditate. Hopefully it was just a hairline fracture and wouldn't need setting.

When her lids fluttered opened a few minutes later, she found herself staring at a pretty blonde woman in scrubs giving her a cool smile. At first she didn't recognize her, but then it clicked.

Courtney Lockhart DeLollis from MeetMyMate.com.

Fabulous.

"Hey, there. How's that ankle feeling?"

"Not awesome," she admitted. How petty that the pain of seeing Courtney manage to look attractive in her olive-green, ill-fitting scrubs was far more acute than the pain in her leg.

"I can imagine. Is Shane here?" Courtney asked, taking the blood pressure cuff from its housing on the wall.

"No, we're…not together."

"I knew that, sorry." She wrapped the cuff around Cat's arm and pumped it up, pressing the stethoscope against the inside of her elbow. "I just saw Lacey and everyone else in the waiting room and wondered if he'd been there, too." The air hissed from the apparatus, and Courtney was silent for a moment before taking the stethoscope from her ears.

"No. I haven't seen him." She bit her tongue to keep from adding, "Have you?"

Courtney handed her a glass and a Dixie cup with two pills in it. "That's just Tylenol for the pain."

Cat took it and washed it down with the tepid water. "Thanks."

"Someone can sit in here with you while you wait. Want me to get your brother?"

"No, thanks. Everyone's fussing all over me, and I just want it quiet."

"No problem. I'll let them know you're doing well and will see them shortly." She tugged the Velcro off and picked up the rest of her gear. "The doctor should be here in just a few minutes to discuss the results of your X-ray." She paused and added in a whisper, "But between me and you, I took a peek at the film, and it's definitely broken. Sorry."

Cat should have cared. Having a cast was going to be damned inconvenient. Especially since she was supposed to have four prototype pieces ready for her boss to see by the end of next week. She didn't do a whole lot of the sewing anymore, so she wasn't worried about the foot pedal, but even getting around was going to be a pain with the bulky cast and crutches. And still, she felt only a twinge of annoyance over it. The thought of Shane leaving made everything else pale in comparison.

She looked up to see Courtney still looking down at her, a thoughtful look marring her pretty face. "We were never together, you know," the other woman said softly. "Not before, and not now. We're just friends, and to be honest, I haven't even talked to him in over a week. He took this thing with you pretty hard."

Some of the tightness in Cat's lungs eased, and she blew out a breath, trying to keep her tone casual. "I appreciate you telling me that, but it's really none of my business. We were never together either. Not really."

"I know. Can I ask why?" There was no judgment in her eyes, just genuine confusion. "I have to admit, it seems so strange to me. Most people spend a lifetime trying to find someone to look at them the way you guys were looking at each other that night at Sully's."

Cat considered blowing her off with a fib, but found the truth pouring from her lips before she could stop it. "I think I'm better alone. I love my career, I love the path I've chosen. I don't want to veer off and wind up taking someone else's path, you know? Shane is so strong. He's a bona fide hero. But I want to have my own life and not just be someone's sidekick."

"So you want a weak guy who will be yours instead?"

"No. I just want…hell, I don't know anymore. All I know is that I don't want to give up my whole identity the way my mother did."

"Are you sure that's the way your mom sees it?"

"I can't imagine how else she could see it. She gave up the thing she loved more than anything to support my dad's career and stay home with us."

Courtney cocked her head and gave her a long, searching look. "Have you ever asked her how she feels about that decision?"

"No." Nor did she want to talk about this anymore. Cat took another sip of water and cleared her throat. "I'm, uh, feeling pretty tired, so I think I'll just close my eyes until the doctor's ready for me."

Courtney hesitated, but then nodded. "Okay. I'll be back to check on you later. One last thought, though. I have years of experience with a controlling guy. The kind of guy who slowly but surely takes over your life, until you feel like you can't even make a decision about what to wear without his help. That's giving up your identity. What your mom did? Not the same. Now I'm terrified of giving up even a piece of myself to anyone again, and it's taken me two years to even get up the courage to try." She held Cat's gaze with a frank stare. "But I think I would have tried with Shane. He's a good man. It's written all over his face and comes through in everything he does. You're a fool if you let him go." She didn't wait for a response before she turned and walked out of the room.

Cat covered her eyes with her hands and groaned. What the hell was she going to do? It had always seemed so clear before. Avoid emotional entanglements. Since Shane, everything had been a muddy mess. She punched her pillow and had just folded it in half under her head when a familiar voice echoed down the hall.

"I'm here for Mary Catherine Thomas, please."

Cat closed her eyes. Mom was here. So much for being left alone with her thoughts.

"I'm sorry, ma'am, but the patient prefers to be alone for the time being." Courtney's tone was polite but firm.

The voice that followed was firmer. "Well that's unfortunate, young lady, because I'm her mother, and she doesn't have a say in the matter."

Cat worked up a smile and sat up right before her mother barreled through the door.

"You're getting too old for this, Mary Catherine. And frankly, so am I." In spite of the bluster, Cat could see the worry on her face.

Courtney stood in the doorway and sent her a questioning look.

"It's fine, she can stay, thanks," Cat said with a nod.

When Courtney left, her mother turned back to assess her ankle with narrowed eyes. "Does it hurt badly?"

"Not too much, no. The doctor will probably put it in a temporary cast to stabilize it and then I'll have to get it casted for real at the orthopedic surgeon's tomorrow or the day after, depending on the swelling."

"I'll drive you."

"I can drive mys—"

"I said, I'll drive you." Fire crackled in her mother's green eyes and Cat knew better than to argue. "Now tell me, what happened out there? Galen said you saw a rabbit?"

"Yeah. Came out of nowhere. I guess I was distracted and before I knew it, I was ass over teakettle."

"You've been riding way too long to make such a rookie mistake. You should have been more aware of your surroundings, and you never swerve for an animal if you don't know what you're swerving into unless it's—"

"Unless it's a bear. I know, Mom."

Kitty's ginger brows gathered into a thunderous frown. "Well if you know so much, missy, tell me what it was that had you so damned distracted that you nearly killed yourself?"

"Just work stuff," she hedged, reaching for her cup of water.

"And Shane." It wasn't a question, which was odd since Cat hadn't told her about the two of them, and Galen wouldn't have said anything…

Suddenly it hit her who would have. "Mrs. Decker. What, did she call you and tell you about us?"

"That's not important. What's important is that the two of you talk and try to work this out. Shane is as unhappy as you are, and for what? Because you're afraid to settle down?"

She quashed the little flutter in her heart and gave her mom the stare-down. "I'm not afraid to settle down, Mom. I like the idea of having one person to come home to." She swallowed hard, Courtney's words playing over in her mind. "What scares me is that I will lose myself completely. Like you did."

Her mother drew back, a frown wrinkling her smooth brow. "What are you talking about?"

"I'm terrified to not have anything of my own and have my happiness dependent on the happiness of everyone around me." She swiped her good arm across her tear-filled eyes and met her mother's stricken gaze. "And I'm scared to wind up with my violin on a shelf in the corner of the study, unplayed, gathering dust."

"Is that what you think of my life?" Kitty's voice shook with emotion. "That I'm some martyr who sacrificed my dreams to marry your father and stay home with you kids?"

Cat moved to stop her. To take it back, because hearing it come from her mother's mouth made it sound so awful, but Kitty held up a hand.

"Answer me. Is that what you think?"

"Kind of." So why did she feel so silly about saying it now? "You always looked so wistful whenever you went into the room and touched that case. Are you going to tell me you didn't compromise and give up what you love for your family? That you didn't change everything for us?"

"I can't believe, all this time, that's what you thought." Regret filled her mother's her face. "I didn't change for you,

Cat. I just…changed. The things I felt were important shifted. Violin will always be a part of who I am. I can still make music whenever I want to. I don't need people to clap for me to feel accomplished. I've had a million other successes, compounded by you and your brother. The sense of pride I feel when Galen wins a fight or you sell a new piece is no less than I would feel if I'd done it myself. And to be honest? The two of you are almost more excitement and adventure than my heart can take." She reached out to pet Cat's hair with a loving hand.

"So you're content with the way your life turned out?"

Kitty shook her head. "No."

Here it came. The bombshell. Cat braced herself for the cold hard truth.

"I'm *happy*. Content is something different. It's passive. I'm actively happy and grateful every day for my life. That I have a good, strong marriage with a man I adore, and two children who are healthy and bright and funny. We get to spend our summers by the lake, and our weekends with our friends and family." She shrugged, her green eyes shiny with tears. "Giving up my career as a violinist wasn't a sacrifice, or even a compromise. It was a choice. *My* choice, so I wouldn't have to be away all the time. I gave up time doing something I loved to spend time doing something I loved even more. Your choices might be different, and that's okay, too. But to deny yourself happiness now so that you're not faced with difficult decisions later? That's not you. That's not on your bucket list. So what are you doing here, love?"

Cat stared at her mother as those words sank in deep. The memory of her mother's violin in the study faded to the background and dozens more battled for center stage. Weekends at the lake fishing for bass, baking cranberry muffins every Sunday, cutting carrots for snowmen's noses, sewing clothes for her teddy bears. Her mother cheering on the sidelines when she'd opted to try out for the boys' basketball team, and sitting in the hospital just like today, holding her hand while she got stitches from an elbow to the chin. She'd always known she'd had a great childhood, but she'd never imagined that those times had been as important to her mother as they had been to her.

Cat pushed, one more time, afraid to grab on to the fragile ribbon of hope curling around her heart. "If you had a time machine, and could go back?"

Kitty shook her head and shrugged. "I wouldn't change a thing."

The truth of it was plain to see on her mother's face, and suddenly the weight she hadn't even known she'd been carrying was suddenly lifted from her shoulders. "What time is it?" she asked Kitty, panic wrestling her newfound elation.

"Four o'clock, why?"

"I've got to get out of here."

Chapter Fourteen

"*Now boarding zone three. Passengers in zone four, please have your tickets out, and prepare to board.*"

Shane stared sightlessly down at the ticket in his hand, wishing he'd booked the flight for later in the week when they'd had first-class seats available. Then he could've kicked back and at least attempted to get some sleep. Flying coach made it near impossible for a guy his size to get comfortable, and that meant wakey-wakey for five and a half hours and probably having to chat with his seatmate. The set of newborn twins seated near the gate window chose that moment to start wailing again, and he winced. They still hadn't boarded yet either, which meant they were likely in his zone.

"Please God, not my row," he muttered.

He loved kids, but he'd been sleeping like shit lately, and his patience was wearing thin. He felt a twinge of guilt and a rush of sympathy for the harried mother. She was there alone, and she was probably dreading this flight way more than he was. He remembered his nieces at that age. Traveling had been a royal bitch for his sister. Nothing at all like just being able to pick up and go like people without kids.

His thoughts made the short trip back to Cat, who seemed to take over most of his brain space when he was awake. Or asleep. Or in between.

Fuck.

He missed her way more than he should. How had she become such a huge piece of him in such a short time? Before that night in Atlantic City, it had been a flickering hope. A chance in hell that maybe she was finally ready for something real. Once he'd had a taste, he was sunk, and now nothing less than everything would do.

He folded the newspaper he'd been reading and tucked it into the pouch of his duffel bag, then stood to sling the bag over his shoulder.

"Now boarding zone four." The intercom blared again, and Shane took a look around to make sure he had all his stuff.

"I don't cook," a soft voice called from behind him.

He paused in his tracks.

"And I clean, but only when I have to."

Shane whipped his head around to see Cat approaching on crutches, with an inflatable cast around her leg. Fear lanced through him.

"Jesus, what happened to y—"

She shook her head furiously, tears filling her green eyes. "It's so not important. The only thing that's important is that you don't go."

"All zones have been called. Any remaining passengers, please board the aircraft bound for LAX at this time."

Cat hobbled closer, pain etched on her face. "I like my freedom, and I sure as shit won't ask your permission to cross stuff off my bucket list. I'm cranky in the morning until I've had my coffee, and I'm not sure I ever want kids." She shifted to her good leg and leaned her crutch against the chair next to him, then laid her hand on his chest. "What I'm trying to say is that, I don't have any idea how to be a good girlfriend. I'm not used to compromising or having someone to answer to or clear my schedule with. And to be honest? It scares the everloving shit out of me. But I want to try. If you do. Because being with you *is* an adventure."

His heart was hammering in his chest, and it took all he had not to scoop her up and run away with her. Take what she was offering and call it good. But she needed to know what she was getting into.

"I don't want to hurt you, Cat, but I don't know if I can be what you need me to be."

Her face fell, and the sadness there threatened to kill him, but she needed to hear him out.

"I love you. I loved you when you dated Alex Michlaus and you snuck out of the house to go for a ride on his motorcycle in the middle of the night. I loved you when you decided that the best way to celebrate your birthday was to jump out of an airplane. I loved you when you moved to New York City at the age of eighteen all by yourself just to take a bite of the Big Apple. All the people who loved you sat by and watched you take life by the balls—terrified for you half the time—but no one ever once tried to hold you back. You're so fearless in a lot of ways, and I admire the hell out of that. We all do. But the other day, at the Abbotts' cottage?"

He set down his bag and covered her hand with his. "I can't say that I wouldn't do something like that again if we were together for real. It's not about control, or making you change, or quashing your spirit. I don't want to do any of that. But there's a line to how much I can take. Maybe I handled it the wrong way, but damn it, all I could think of at that moment was trying to save you the pain of seeing that little girl. So I can't promise you that I won't try talk you out of something, or worry about you, or at least expect to be there to pick up the pieces with you when you fall. Because you're a fucking whirlwind, an—"

"Shh," she whispered, relief softening her features. She squeezed his fingers tight. "You don't have to explain. I get it now. And it took me some time to admit to myself that it goes both ways. I thought about that night so many times and, in spite of my stubbornness, I don't know if I would have done any different in your shoes. Because I love you, too."

Relief coursed through him, and he bent low to brush his lips over hers, but she pulled away.

"That doesn't mean I'd react any differently if you tried to pull that shit again, though," she warned with a smile. "I would bitch and complain, maybe throw something smashy for effect, then we'd have to scrap it out before we had super-sweaty make-up sex."

Damn if super-sweaty make-up sex didn't sound good.

"Last call for flight two-three-seven."

Shane pulled away and shook his head slowly. "Shit. Cat, I've got to go."

She drew back, her face going pale. "You're…you're still going to leave?" she asked, her voice trembling.

He tugged her close into his chest. "I have to. I've got to get all my stuff."

She pulled away and gaped at him. "Wait. I thought you were going back to California for good?"

He shook his head slowly. "Of course not. I just had to go back for a week to pack up my apartment and arrange to have my stuff shipped here."

"But your mom said you were leaving, and…" She trailed off and then a light went off and she grinned. "Oh, well played, Martha. Well played."

Shane leaned back to kiss her nose. "My mom bamboozled you, huh? That doesn't surprise me in the least. In fact, I have to admit, for the first time in my life, I'm actually glad she's such a busybody. I'd have had to suffer another week before I came back and put my new plan into motion."

"What plan?"

He stepped back and dug through his duffel to pull out a small box. "You didn't think I was just going to let you walk away, did you?"

Her gazed was locked on the box. "What the fuck is that?" she demanded, the abject terror in her eyes almost enough to make him laugh out loud.

"Not what you think. But I'm going to take a knee anyway." He crouched down and knelt before her. "I'd hoped that when I came back for good and you had a little more time to cool off, I'd be able to get you back. Then I was going to let you get used to the idea before I asked, but now feels right. Cat," he opened the box and in it was nestled a folded piece of paper, "I know it's a pretty big step, but will you help me complete my bucket list?"

She blew out a sigh of relief and gave him a blinding smile. "Yes. Totally, one hundred percent yes. Jeez, you scared me there for a second. Not that someday…"

He stood and pulled her close. "Baby steps," he whispered into her hair.

"Baby steps," she agreed, nodding against his chest.

A heavyset agent approached them, scowling. "Sir, are you boarding this flight or not? The doors close in two minutes."

Shit, everything was going so well, he didn't want to leave her now. "You know what, I can rebook in a couple weeks and—"

"Or, I can go with you if you want some company?" Cat reached into her pocket and pulled out a wrinkled ticket. "I had to buy one because they wouldn't let me through security without it."

"Hell yes, I want company." He moved to pull her in for

another squeeze but she held up a hand.

"I can only stay a couple days because I have work, but at least we can be together. And you'd have to take me to the doctor to get a cast, and let me borrow some clothes."

"Or not," he murmured, letting his gaze slide down her body.

"Or not," she agreed, a wicked gleam lighting her eyes.

"Come on, lovebirds, we doing this or what?" the agent asked.

"Yeah," Cat murmured softly, never taking her eyes off him. "Yeah, we are so doing this."

Acknowledgments

Thanks to my amazing husband for being my greatest fan and for convincing me that I actually might be able to do this for real. As always, thanks to Kerri-Leigh Grady for being the fruit in my pie, the cream in my coffee, and the tequila in my sunrise. You are the bestest editor ever. And, last but not least, thanks to Liz Pelletier for making dreams come true. 'Nuff said.

About the Author

USA TODAY bestselling author Christine Bell is one half of the happiest couple in the world. She doesn't like clowns or bugs (except ladybugs, on account of their cute outfits), but loves movies, football, and playing Texas Hold 'Em. Writing is her passion, but if she had to pick another occupation, she'd be a wizard. She loves writing fun, sexy contemporary romances, but also hopes to one day publish something her dad can read without wanting to dig his eyes out with rusty spoons. Christine loves to hear from her readers. Visit her on her website, Twitter, and Facebook.

Discover the rest of the **Dare Me** *series...*

Down for the Count

Down the Aisle

Down on Her Knees

Also by Christine Bell

Perfectly Matched series

Dirty Trick

Dirty Deal

For Hire series

Wife for Hire

Guardian for Hire

Reforming the Rock Star

Holding out for a Hero

Little White Lie

Conned

If you love sexy romance, one-click these steamy Brazen releases...

HARD COMPROMISE
a *Compromise Me* novel by Samanthe Beck

Laurie Peterson assumes her impulsive one-night stand with sinfully sexy Sheriff Ethan Booker is the biggest surprise of the year...until her bakery burns down while she's basking in the afterglow. It looks like her dreams are up in smoke, but then Ethan proposes a deal too tempting to resist.

A FOOL FOR YOU
a *Foolproof Love* novel by Katee Robert

It's been thirteen years since Hope Moore left Devil's Falls, land of sexy cowboys and bad memories. Back for the weekend, she has no intention of seeing Daniel Rodriguez, the man she never got over, or for the two of them getting down and dirty. It's just a belated goodbye, right? No harm, no foul. Until six weeks later, when her pregnancy test comes back positive...

WOUND TIGHT
a *Made in Jersey* novel by Tessa Bailey

When CEO Renner Bastion walks into a room, everyone keeps their distance. Well, everyone but the sarcastic, tattooed, Boston-bred security guard whose presence has kept Renner in New Jersey longer than intended. As if the unwanted attraction isn't unsettling enough, Renner finds out Milo isn't as unavailable as originally thought. Worse, his protector is looking for lessons in how to seduce another man. Lessons only Renner can give him.

Made in United States
Troutdale, OR
04/27/2025